See Her

a novel by Jane Conquest

for Sebastian

Cover art by Isabel Burke Copyright © 2018.

Instagram: @the.flightless.artist

table of contents

ice cream

In a world of color, we sometimes find ourselves overlooking things.

If I'd paid more attention, I might have noticed her sooner; maybe out on the sidewalk, or somewhere in the halls at school. I mean, once I saw her, I really *saw* her; the kind of seeing that you never forget. Never.

We met in an ice cream shop.

It wasn't a formal meeting. A girl came in, her hair billowing around her like a soft purple cloud, and tossed her designer bag at a nearby booth like she owned the place. From there, she strutted right up to the counter and locked eyes with me, a pearly-white grin opening up between her thin lips.

"Two small vanillas, please," she said, knocking once on the counter. My eyes flickered briefly to the brown-haired girl standing just behind her, then back up to her face, where I found her still grinning.

"Let me guess," I said, leaning back against the counter as I dried the freshly-washed scooper with a towel. "Your favorite color is... red?"

She laughed then, a loud, booming laugh that bounced off the walls and drew glances from the other patrons in the shop, and I felt proud for having produced such a lovely sound from such a lovely face. I cracked a sly smile as I dug the scooper down into the soft, sweet ice cream, rolling four perfect scoops into two separate cups.

After a moment, I paused, glancing around to make sure Sara was still holed up in the back room. "I'm not really supposed to do this, but..." I reached beneath the counter and pulled out a small jar of purple

1

sprinkles, tilting the contents over the cup of vanilla like a dark rain, "Free topping. On the house."

The purple-haired girl's ever-present grin grew wider, and she nudged the girl behind her, who took a step back. Returning my focus to the purple-haired girl's dark eyes, I handed over the two cups.

"What do we owe you?" She asked, reaching into her pocket.

"Eight for the two," I said, waiting for them both to finish digging out their money. They forked over two fives, and I rounded the cash register to punch in their order, my eyes glancing up briefly to meet with the purple-haired girl's.

"Thanks," she said as she accepted their change, waving her friend in the direction of the booth. When I noticed the purple-haired girl still hadn't left the counter, I looked up expectantly. "Er... is this always your shift?" She asked, twirling a violet strand around her finger. She seemed nervous, completely different from the confident supermodel from just a moment before.

"Yeah," I told her. "Mondays, Tuesdays, and Thursdays."

The smile returned. "Great," she said, then turned to leave. "Thanks again."

"No problem," I called after her, watching her join her friend at the table. I kept watching as they finished their ice cream, kept watching as the purple-haired girl's echoing laughter trailed out through the front door, and kept watching as they climbed into a white pickup truck, then pulled out of the parking lot.

It was in that ice cream shop that I met the love of my life.

gift

She started coming back regularly.

Sometimes the girl with the brown hair would be with her, sometimes not. I preferred when she was alone, free to spark up a conversation over vanilla ice cream with purple sprinkles. I began to take notice of her outfits; one day she'd be wearing band tees and skirts, the next a simple tank top and jeans. Sometimes her violet hair would be tied up into two buns, or hanging loose around her shoulders. There was something different about her each time she visited, whether it be her lipstick color, or her earrings, or her outfit, and I liked that.

I decided to ask Sara if she came around when I wasn't here, and was pleased to know she'd been by only one time in my absence, when Julia was working.

"Now leave me alone," Sara said, shooing me out of the back room as she hunched over yet another stack of paperwork. "Do you know how many customers we get? I don't have time to look out for each and every one."

I left smiling.

A few weeks after we first met, the purple-haired girl invited me to sit with her at a booth in the corner of the shop. I took an early lunch and joined her, bringing the usual for her, and taking a medium chocolate for myself. As we ate, I noticed her spoonfuls were precise and certain, swirling the ice cream around in order to find the perfect mouthful.

"Listen, Aaron," she said, her eyes finding the table. "I know your name, but I realized you don't know mine."

"That's true," I said to her. "It'd be nice to stop calling you 'miss' if you're going to be eating ice cream here three times a week. How long do you plan to keep this up before diabetes set in, anyway?"

She giggled, and an involuntary smile crept up my face. I'd never heard her giggle before. "Yeah, well, my name's Taylor. It's actually my middle name, but I prefer it."

"What's your first name?" I asked casually.

"Ah-ah. I'm not sure if we're on a secret-first-name basis yet."

I snorted, nearly choking on my ice cream. "Fine, then. Taylor it is."

And Taylor she was.

***

We celebrated her seventeenth birthday together in September, right when school was starting. My hours would be changing soon, and we both knew it, but skirted around the topic as much as humanly possible.

"You're officially a junior," I announced grandly, presenting her with a pint of vanilla ice cream and a wrapped gift box. "Ice cream's free of charge. I paid for it."

"It's a sad day when the guy from the ice cream shop gets you more presents than your friends," Taylor joked, accepting her gifts from my outstretched hands.

"Hey, I'm not just *any* guy." I tapped my name tag. "I'm Aaron."

"Can I open this now?" She asked, raising her eyes to the clock. "Your break started three minutes ago. Come around from the counter."

"Will do," I said, hanging my apron on its hook, then joining her by the tip jar. "Let's take this to a table, shall we?"

When we'd settled in at our usual booth in the corner, I waited expectantly as she unwrapped her gift. She pulled the paper back to reveal a cardboard box.

"If you say the 'a box! Just what I wanted!' joke, I will shoot you in the face," I said lightly.

"With what, an ice cream scooper?" She bantered, smiling mischievously. "Face it, Aaron, you're about as threatening as that old lady that comes in here every Tuesday."

"I'll have you know that Gretchen was once a WWE fighter."

"Is that so?" Taylor grinned as she pulled back the folds, her eyes widening in surprise. "A t-shirt!"

"Your one with the Beatles was looking pretty raggedy," I told her, watching her unfold it and hold it up against her thin body. "Did you wear it, what, every day since the seventh grade?"

"I threw it out last week," she murmured, turning the shirt around to look at the back. "It's perfect. Thank you."

"Wait," I said, holding up my arms to stop her from putting it back in the box. "There's more."

She peered down inside, then grinned.

"Purple sprinkles," she exclaimed happily, pulling out the brand-new jar.

"To go with your ice cream, of course," I said.

cell phone

Taylor went out of town the week before school started, so she gave me her phone number.

"We've lost nearly half our revenue without you around," I said into my cell, simultaneously juggling milkshakes for an entire family. "Hold on—" I covered the end and mouthed '*sorry*' to the customers as I rang up their credit card, "—okay, I'm back."

"You'd think with how many free toppings you've given me that you would actually be *gaining* revenue," Taylor countered.

"Shh!" I cupped my hands around the receiver. "The police might be *listening*."

"Oh, yes. Because they're going to bust down your door and arrest you for purple sprinkle distribution, you *monster*."

"I have to go," I said, glancing up at Sara as she approached. "I'll call you back on my break."

"I'll be here."

"Bye." I hung up the phone, slipping it in my pocket as I turned to face Sara. "Emerging from your lair, boss?"

"Ha-ha, that cute boy charm might work on teenaged girls, but not me." She crossed her arms over her chest. "Personal phone calls are prohibited during working hours."

"Won't happen again," I assured her. When she didn't move, I sighed. "Come on, Sara, you *know* me."

"I'll let you off just this once, but there will be consequences if I catch you again," she warned, sternly staring me down.

"Gotcha. Now, shoo. You've got work to do." I looked over at where a party bus of kids had just walked in through the door. "And so do I."

***

"Was the ice cream in New York as good as ours?" I asked Taylor, sliding her usual order across the counter. It was good to have her back, but I didn't say so.

"Oh, it's not even a *competition*," Taylor said, her grin widening at my nasty glare, "...New York *sucked*."

"Phew," I gasped dramatically. "You had me worried there."

"Let's sit," she told me, nodding her head at our booth.

"Can't, sorry," I said, glancing over at the clock. "My break's not for ten minutes, and I already got in trouble for talking to you on the phone."

"Oh, come on," she groaned. "Your boss won't care. It's a ghost town in here, anyway."

I chewed on my lower lip, deliberating.

"Fine," I caved. "But this was *your* idea, alright?"

"Fair," she said, following me to the corner. "So, spill. What exciting things happened while I was away?"

"I got a tooth pulled."

"Too much ice cream."

"Says *you*. I see you got your hair redyed."

"Yep, roots were starting to grow in." She grimaced. "It'd be better if I had dark natural hair, but, since I'm blonde, it just looked like someone spilled soda on my head."

"I'm sure it wasn't noticeable."

"You would know. You see me more than anyone nowadays."

"Yeah, and about that," I began, rubbing the back of my neck, "how would you like to..." I trailed off, feeling a hot blush begin to creep up my face. "Maybe... get coffee, or something? I mean, I'd sure hate to be the cause of your addiction to ice cream..."

"Coffee sounds great," she interrupted, and I immediately relaxed. "When do you wanna go?"

I'd just opened my mouth to respond when a shadow fell over the table. I looked up, my stomach plummeting down into my feet.

"Sara," I murmured, trying to appear casual. "What a pleasant surprise."

"Break's not for five minutes, Aaron, and it looks like you've been here for a while." She narrowed her eyes at Taylor's half-eaten cup, and I swallowed.

"I'm sorry," Taylor piped up, setting her spoon down on the table. "It was my idea. My fault." I glanced over at her, impressed, as Sara spoke.

"I don't care whose idea it was," Sara snapped, her brows drawing together. "Ever since you've started coming in here, Aaron's been slacking on his work."

"Hey, I'm right here," I said. "I'm sorry, okay? We both are."

Sara frowned. "I hate to say this, but there are lots of people who'd love to have your job."

I blinked, dreading her next words.

"Aaron, the next time you slack off, you're fired."

barbecue

Taylor didn't come on Thursday.

My shift came and went, but I held out hope until the very last minute that she'd show up. It was only when I went to hang my apron up for the day that I started to get concerned.

I called her phone, but it went straight to voicemail. When I called a second time, the line was picked up, but there was nothing but silence on her end.

"Hey," I said. Still nothing. "Taylor?"

"Where are you right now?" She asked, and my shoulders sagged at the sound of her voice.

"Walking down the sidewalk from the shop," I said. "I'm on my way home, why?"

"Get in."

A familiar white pickup truck zoomed around the corner and screeched to a stop beside me. I was so stunned that I didn't even lower the phone from my ear.

Taylor, staring at me from the driver's seat, repeated into her cell, "get *in*."

I snapped back to reality, hurrying around the side of the car, then sliding into the passenger's seat.

"Taylor?" I asked, buckling my seatbelt.

"Let's drive," she said, slamming her foot on the gas.

***

We drove out of town and began to cruise along the countryside, counting cows that we passed and pointing out pretty beds of flowers.

"Taylor, I gotta ask," I said, turning to look at where her attention was fixed on the horizon, "where were you today?"

She sighed. "I didn't want to get you in trouble."

"You wouldn't have, I—"

"I just have a tendency to get people in trouble," she mumbled, barely audible. "I'm kind of... reckless. I don't think. I didn't... *don't* want to make the same mistake again."

My face softened. "It's really all right," I told her. "Sara has good days and bad days. She owns the entire ice cream chain, so she's always stressed out."

Taylor said nothing. Unhappy with her silence, I went on:

"Don't worry about it. Really."

Taylor chewed on her lip for a moment. "Let's get something to eat," she said finally, and I sat back in my seat. I still wasn't convinced that she was reassured, but decided to let the matter drop for now. "You like barbecue?"

"It's all I live on."

"Perfect. There's a place up ahead."

A few minutes later, we pulled into the parking lot of a rustic restaurant proudly boasting its name, *Cuidado*, in an enormous neon sign above the entrance. Taylor hopped out of the truck and headed for the doorway, her keys jingling from her fingers as she went. I followed.

"Table for two, please," Taylor told the hostess, glancing back at me. We were soon seated in a worn booth near the front, surrounded by authentic Texan merchandise and mementos. Our waitress was a beach-blonde woman with pigtails and a shirt that was tied up into one of those weird bow things I never quite understood, and she had a deep southern accent I could barely interpret.

"How're y'all doin' today?" She asked, not waiting for our answer before setting two menus down in front of us. "Mah name's Cindy and I'll be helpin' y'all out tonight, can I start'cha off with some dranks?"

"Water for me," I told her.

"Same here, but no lemon," Taylor said, her eyes following Cindy as she nodded, then headed towards the kitchen.

"You don't like lemon in your water?" I asked, a teasing smile working its way onto my face. Taylor turned back to me, a flicker of her old self showing through for a moment.

"Guess I've got more of a sweet tooth," she said, then grew serious. "Look, again, I just wanted you to know how sorry I am for Tuesday."

"Stop apologizing," I told her, waving my hand dismissively. "Everything's fine."

"It's *not*, though," she said, sitting on her hands. She bowed her head over the table. "You've been so nice to me, and all I've done is cause trouble."

"Taylor—"

"Don't give me free sprinkles anymore. I want to pay for them."

"If that's what you want, then—"

"And I'll start coming around right when your break starts, so I won't be tempted to pull you away any sooner."

I smiled as she went on, chattering nonstop about the rights and wrongs of things.

Finally interrupting, I held up my hand to silence her. "How about we do this more often, too?" I suggested, gesturing around to the bustling restaurant. "Hanging outside of my work. School's starting soon, and we'll be busy with that, but I'll be working less." I smiled at her. "Sound good?"

She grinned softly. "You really are a great guy, Aaron."

"One of my many perfections," I bantered, watching her twirl her purple hair around her finger. "Let's talk about something else, now."

"My real name is Anna," Taylor told me, her eyes scanning over the restaurant. "And where is that damn waitress?"

<u>clara</u>

I started seeing Taylor more regularly, but she still visited me every day I worked at the shop, which changed to Tuesdays and Wednesdays after school, as well as Saturday mornings.

"Maybe we can request a schedule change," Taylor was saying as she watched me pour purple sprinkles into her cup of ice cream. "For chemistry, or cooking, or something." She glanced up at me as I handed over her order. "You're taking cooking class too, right?"

"Gotta branch out from ice cream eventually," I chirped lightly as I accepted her five-dollar bill. "You're going to be broke if you keep this up, Taylor Anna."

"I told you not to call me that. And anyway, I've got nothing else to spend my money on, so why not?"

"Can I take you out tonight?"

"I was actually thinking you could come have dinner at my house," she suggested, leaning on the counter as I began washing the scooper. "Both my parents are in town, so it's a special occasion."

"They work a lot?"

"Oh, like you wouldn't *believe*. Did I ever tell you about the firm they run?"

"Nope."

"It's like a sort of medical software distributor, or some shit like that. It's all so complicated, I have no idea how they gave birth to an airhead like me."

"Hey now, come on. You're the smartest girl in cooking class, by far."

She leaned across the counter to punch my shoulder. "Shut up," she growled, grinning. "So, what do you think? You in?"

"Yeah, I'll let my folks know when I get off work," I told her, glancing over at the customers that had just walked in. "You'll pick me up?"

"I'll be here," she promised, backing away towards the door. "See you at 7:30."

"7:30," I echoed.

***

At 7:35, I was sitting in the passenger seat of Taylor's white pickup truck, watching her steer us out of the parking lot of the shop.

"We have to make a quick detour," she told me apologetically. "I gotta pick my little sister up from the park."

"I didn't know you had a little sister," I said, surprised.

"You've seen her, like, a billion times, silly," she chastised. "You know, the short one, with the brown hair."

"Oh, her. I thought she was your friend."

"Well, we're Irish twins, so the age difference isn't much," she explained, letting go of the wheel to push her violet hair out of her face. "She's been through some shit, and she's shy, so will you at least *try* to be nice to her?"

"What's that tone for?" I demanded, laughing. "When have I ever been anything but charming?" I looked out the window. "What's she doing all the way out here, anyway?"

"She spends a lot of time by herself." Taylor paused, chewing on her lip. "I don't think she has any friends."

"That's incredibly doubtful, given that she's *your* sister."

"How many friends can I have if I spend all my time with the ice cream boy?"

"Touché."

We pulled into a dirt lot facing a rickety-looking playground, where I spied a small figure sitting on the swings with her back to us. I could see the thin cord of a pair earbuds trailing up to her ears, and she appeared to be hunched over something in her lap.

Taylor opened the driver's door and stepped halfway out of the car. "Hey!" she shouted. "Let's go!"

The girl's shoulders went rigid, her hair flying around as she twisted in her seat to look at us. She quickly hopped off the swing, grabbed a brown messenger bag from where it had been lying beside her on the ground, then trudged towards the car. I could now see she had been writing in a hardcover notebook, a pen sticking out of the top as a bookmark. The girl clutched the notebook to her chest as she rounded the car and opened the door to the seat behind me, tossing her things to the other side of the car before climbing inside.

"Aaron, this is my little sister Clara," Taylor said, gesturing between the two of us. "Clara, this is Aaron."

"Nice to meet you," I said, turning my head to try and look at the small girl in the backseat.

"Hi," Clara peeped, reaching for her earbuds.

"Don't get all plugged in yet," Taylor ordered her, and Clara dropped the earbuds like they were hot, folding her hands in her lap as she stared down at her shoes. "Aaron's going to be eating dinner with us tonight."

Clara said nothing, so I spoke. "I'm really excited to meet your parents," I said. "I heard they own a medical firm?"

"You work at the ice cream shop, right?" Clara asked softly, barely audible. I opened my mouth, glanced at Taylor, then closed it.

"That's right," Taylor answered for me, driving out of the lot. "I've been going over there a lot lately, to keep him company."

"Mom and dad won't like that," Clara whispered, her shoulders hiking up, and Taylor's brow drew together into a line.

"Plug in, little runt," she growled, and Clara immediately pounced on her earbuds, sticking them into the jack of a small iPhone. "Mom and dad are going to love Aaron. Right?"

"Right," Clara murmured noncommittally, pulling out her notebook to resume her writing.

The rest of the drive was spent in silence, one thought ringing out clear in my mind.

That was weird.

dinner

At 8:15, we arrived at the house, which I discovered to be a comfortable two-story building with neatly-trimmed hedges and a wooden porch. It seemed like any average suburban home, and, as I looked at Taylor, I realized I couldn't picture someone as extraordinary as her coming from a place like this.

Clara, maybe. She had medium-length chestnut brown hair, thin and wispy, always hanging low in her face. She never raised her eyes above the ground, and her full lips seemed to be set in a permanent line.

After climbing out of the car, I followed Taylor and Clara into the house, waiting in the doorway as they both peeled off their hoodies.

"Mom! We're home!" Taylor called. I swore Clara's head drooped even lower as a blonde woman rounded the corner into the entryway, her brows knit in a tight line. She wore a gray tank top and black shorts, her strong arms balled into fists at her sides.

"Where were you?" The woman demanded, glowering at Taylor before turning her nasty expression onto me. "And who's this?"

"This is Aaron, mom," Taylor said. "I told you he'd be coming tonight."

Taylor's mom broke their stare for a moment to offer me a forced, tight-lipped smile. "You most certainly did not," she growled between her teeth. "I would have changed clothes."

"Mom, you look *fine*," Taylor assured her, and both Clara and the woman's shoulders stiffened. I was still hanging around the open doorway, awkward and confused, feeling out of place.

"Aaron, you can call me Mrs. Lawson," Taylor's mom said, wringing her hands in front of her. "Please come inside."

I stepped fully into the house and shut the door behind me, turning my back on the three women as I took off my jacket. "How do you know Aaron?" Mrs. Lawson asked in a hushed whisper.

"He works at the ice cream shop on Pine Street. It's where I've been going for the past few weeks."

Mrs. Lawson scoffed, something unidentifiable in her tone, and my brow furrowed. Taylor hadn't told her parents about me, or even the ice cream shop?

"Where does he go to school?" Mrs. Lawson demanded.

"Gunnison, same as me. Can you chill out, please? We've known each other for a solid month, so I thought it was time he met you guys."

I glanced over my shoulder to watch Mrs. Lawson fold her arms across her chest, eyeing her daughter suspiciously. I'd never seen a parent more alienated from her child than Mrs. Lawson was with Taylor in that moment; it was almost as if I were witnessing an interrogation session.

"He has good manners," Mrs. Lawson noted. My head quickly snapped back around to the coatrack, knowing I wasn't a part of the conversation. "All right, then. Clara, go set the table. Taylor, you take Aaron upstairs, and wash up."

"Fine," Taylor mumbled. The group scattered, Taylor tugging my wrist in the direction of a nearby staircase. Mrs. Lawson hurried off to the kitchen, and didn't look back. After I came to the top of the stairs, I headed over to where Taylor had disappeared into a nearby bathroom.

I stepped up next to her at the sink, and couldn't hold it in any longer. "That was... different."

"Yeah, sorry about that," Taylor mumbled, focusing intently on scrubbing at her hands. "She's just..." I waited for her to finish, but she trailed off and stayed quiet, so I washed my hands and followed her back downstairs, hoping that the tense atmosphere had passed.

After all, I still had to meet Mr. Lawson.

***

Even as Taylor and Clara's mother began to carry out the plates of food, the seat at the head of the table remained unoccupied. I glanced over at Taylor, trying to catch her eye, but she had her gaze fixed on her food, so I looked away, smoothing down the wrinkles on my pants.

Right as we began to eat, a middle-aged man appeared in the doorway to the dining room, his undone tie hanging around his neck. He wore a white button-up shirt and dark gray slacks, evidently a work outfit.

"Ah, smells delicious," the man, presumably Mr. Lawson, said cheerily. "How are you, honey?"

"Fine," Mrs. Lawson barked sharply, focusing on serving herself from a bowl of spaghetti.

"I see we have a guest," Mr. Lawson went on, taking a seat at the head of the table. "And what's your name, young man?"

"Aaron," I told him politely, accepting the bowl from Mrs. Lawson's hands. "Aaron Parker, sir."

"Well, it's very nice to meet you, Aaron Parker," Mr. Lawson said, and I grinned. Finally, some pleasantness.

"I'm sorry I didn't tell you Aaron was coming," Taylor mumbled suddenly, and I stopped, turning my head to look at her. She was still looking down at her untouched food, presumably addressing Mrs. Lawson. "I thought I did. I guess I forgot."

Silence.

"That's all right," Mrs. Lawson finally said, resuming the process of loading her plate. She looked at me, and smiled. "We're happy to have you, Aaron."

"That we are," Mr. Lawson chimed in. He reached for his glass of red wine. "I propose a toast: to Mr. Aaron Parker."

"To Aaron," Mrs. Lawson agreed, but Taylor and Clara stayed silent.

***

The rest of the meal passed uneventfully, ending with me helping Mrs. Lawson wash the dishes in the kitchen.

"You're a very sweet young man," Mrs. Lawson said approvingly, though it was clear she was still stressed out, for whatever reason. "I forget my manners, sometimes. Some of the people Taylor brings home... well, they aren't like you."

"It's been very nice to see you all," I told her earnestly, drying my hands on a nearby towel. "I should be heading out, though."

Mrs. Lawson followed me into the dining room, where Taylor stood from her chair, finally raising her eyes to her mother's.

"I'm gonna drive Aaron home," Taylor told Mrs. Lawson, keeping a good five feet between the two of them. "I'll be back in a little while."

Mrs. Lawson didn't reply until I'd followed Taylor out into the entryway, when she then called, "thank you for coming, Aaron."

"Thanks for having me," I said back, holding the door open for Taylor. I closed it behind us as we stepped out into the chilly September night, draping my jacket over my arm as I joined Taylor on the porch.

"Is something going on?" I dared to ask, leaning over to try and catch her gaze. "Is it always like that in there?"

"Sometimes," Taylor murmured vaguely, then slipped around me to head down the driveway.

I watched her go for a moment before following her, more confused than ever.

tutoring

"My relationship with my family is... difficult," Taylor's crackly voice murmured through the phone. "I'm sorry you got caught in the middle like that."

"It's no problem," I assured her, leaning back against the couch cushions. "I worry about you, though."

"You shouldn't. I won't take you back there again, anyway."

"That's a shame," I said, but was inwardly relieved. "Your sister seemed nice. Just a bit introverted."

"A *bit*?" Taylor chuckled. "That's an understatement. Her best friend is that journal of hers, and she's failing, like, all her classes in school. You'd think with how often she's alone she'd find *some* time to study."

"I could tutor her," I offered. "Which subject does she have the most trouble with?"

"Hm, let's see..." Taylor paused, thinking. "I remember my mom yelling at her about biology the other day."

"Perfect. I just so happen to be an expert biology-ologist."

"I sincerely hope you're joking."

"When am I ever not?"

"I'll text you her number. Don't try to call her – she hates talking on the phone."

24

"Aye aye, captain."

"Did you just—"

"Bye, Taylor."

I hung up, a smile playing on my lips, and waited for Taylor's message.

A moment later, a ten-digit number appeared, shortly followed by a smiley face and an ice cream emoji. I sent her a smiley back and created a new contact for Clara, typing in a short message:

Hey Clara, it's Aaron, Taylor's friend from the other night. She gave me your number, and I was wondering if you'd be up for a tutoring session for biology. You can pick the time and place, I'm flexible. Let me know! -Aaron.

I didn't normally word my texts so formally, let alone sign my name, but Clara gave off the impression that she was rigid in nature – flawless wording, impeccable grammar, that sort of thing.

She responded less than a minute later.

what did she tell you

Swing and a miss. No capital W or question mark. I decided to relax on the properness in order to connect with her more easily.

She told me u were having a bit of trouble. That true?

I sat back, nervously drumming my fingers on my legs. For whatever reason, it was important to me that I made a good impression on Taylor's family, although it was clear they weren't the most open-minded of people.

yeah

I smiled.

I'll make it fun, promise. Where do u want to go?

idk

We could go 2 the park. Would u like that?

ok

Does today work?

what time

2ish?

ok

I found it fitting that Clara typed in all lowercase letters, almost the equivalent to how softly she spoke in real life.

Can Taylor drive u?

ill ask

...

she said yes

Great. See u @ 2.

bye

I sat back, pleased.

Now to review a year's worth of biology.

***

I met Clara at the park, when she pulled up with Taylor in the truck, who waved to me, then sped off. Since I didn't have a car, I'd had my mom drop me off at 1:45, and had been waiting for nearly an hour when Clara finally trudged across the dirty grass towards where I was sitting on the swing set.

"Let's sit over there," I suggested, gesturing at a nearby park bench. Clara nodded, her hair hiding her face, and followed me to where I sat down on the rough wood, moving aside to make room for her. As soon as she set her messenger bag down, she curled in on herself, appearing smaller than ever next to me. "Biology?" I asked, and she nodded, but still made no move for her bag.

I sat back, waiting. "Do you want to play a game first, or something?" I asked.

She shook her head.

"Well, then..." I began, but she cut me off.

"You don't have to do that," she peeped. I stopped, absorbing her words.

"Do what?" I asked.

"Talk to me like I'm a fourth grader."

I was stunned. "I wasn't trying—"

"Yeah, I know," she murmured, hugging her arms around her. "Just remember that two months out of the year Taylor and I are both seventeen."

My mouth opened, then shut. I hadn't thought about that before. "I knew you two were Irish twins, I just didn't—"

"I'm a grade below her, and a foot smaller," Clara went on, still refusing to meet my gaze. "I get it."

There was silence. I had no idea what to say.

After a long pause, Clara reached into her backpack and pulled out a white binder covered in scribbles. As if on autopilot, I slowly reached into my pocket and grabbed the pen and highlighter I'd brought, still keeping my eyes on Clara.

Then we began to work.

"So, how'd you like Clara?" Taylor asked, swirling her spoon in its cup of vanilla. It was Saturday, and Taylor was visiting me at the ice cream shop.

"She's..." I began, then trailed off. Taylor smiled softly.

"I know," she murmured, looking down at her lap. "How did she... what did she say?"

I shrugged. "She thought I was talking down to her."

Taylor's lips formed a line. "Yeah, she's sensitive about that kind of thing. Kids used to pick on her for always being smaller than everyone. She was a preemie, you know."

"I could have guessed," I admitted, running my hands through my hair. "Do you mind if I ask... did something happen to her? You mentioned earlier that she'd been through some shit, but I didn't know if that meant—"

"I can't tell you anything," Taylor cut me off, gently but firmly. "Family rule. If Clara wants to talk about it, you have to hear from her."

I was quiet. "'It'?" I finally questioned, but Taylor shook her head.

"Also, you have to get comfortable with her before asking," she advised. "If you ask too soon, she'll clam up. It's pretty rocky territory with that one."

"Let's talk about something else, then," I suggested. "How's school going?"

"I learned how to make macaroni in cooking the other day," Taylor told me, scraping her cup to get at the last bits of ice cream.

"The most important lesson for college," I joked, and was surprised when Taylor's shoulders went noticeably tense, her head dropping back down to her lap. My brow furrowed. "You're not planning on going to college?"

"No, I..." she kept her mouth open, and I could tell she was thinking hard, "...am. I am going to college. I just haven't applied anywhere yet."

I sat back. "Well, that's totally okay," I assured her. "I mean, junior year *just* started. Do you have any idea of where you're going, though?"

"Maybe Alabama."

"That's good," I said encouragingly, noting the way she was closing in on herself more and more with every passing word.

"What about you?" Taylor asked, finally looking up. "What do you think you'll major in?"

"I'm hoping to get in somewhere on a football scholarship," I told her, taking her empty cup and tossing it at a nearby trashcan. "I have some places in mind, but it doesn't really matter. I'll play football, and major in astronomy, or something like that. I really like space."

"Space," Taylor echoed, smiling. "Like, the stars?"

"No, like '*Blank Space*', the hit song by Taylor Swift."

She laughed then, and I felt myself smiling, too. There was no better sound than Taylor Lawson's laughter.

***

I was spending Saturday night at home, by myself, when my phone buzzed on the coffee table.

I picked it up, frowning at the unknown number.

Hey, is this Aron?

I typed a reply.

It's Aaron, but yes. Who's this?

Levi, 2nd period chemistry. I'm trying out 4 the team in a week.

O, congrats man. Hope you u get it, it's pretty competitive after sophomore yr.

Listen, me & the guys wanted 2 know if u could come 2 a party 2night. Whole team's gonna b there, last binge b4 the season starts. U in?

I sat back, deliberating. After looking around the empty house, I decided I had nothing else to do.

I'm in.

party

At around 10:30 PM, I pulled into the driveway of the address Levi had texted to me, staring up at the neon lights pouring out of the expansive mansion in front of me. Cars were lined up and down the block, but I'd managed to squeeze my mom's small MINI Cooper in near the house, where I could feel loud bass reverberating through the air even inside the car.

Climbing out of the driver's side, I slipped my keys into my pocket, then headed across the lush, freshly-mowed lawn. Despite the few Solo cups littered about, it was clear the owners of the house kept their property neat and tidy, and were well-off enough to do so.

"Aaron!" I turned and spied Levi near the side of the house, waving his arm frantically. "Get over here!"

Smiling politely, I jogged over to where he was standing near a crowd gathered around a beer keg, curious eyes turning to me as I approached.

"Everyone, this is Aaron," Levi introduced me, slapping an arm around my shoulders, despite me being half a foot taller than him. "Word around the keg is that my boy here might be a candidate for team captain this season." Half the people there already knew me as a member of the football team, but Levi seemed too tipsy to notice.

I blushed modestly. "I don't know about that," I said.

Levi wrinkled his nose at me. "Grab a beer, man! Enjoy yourself!"

I nodded, slipped through a few underclassmen swaying heavily on their feet, and grabbed a Solo cup from the stack set up beside the keg.

"Hey, um, Aaron," a boy named Devon muttered, glancing around nervously. "Any idea when the team'll be doing drug tests this year?"

"No idea," I told him truthfully, looking at him over the rim of my cup. "They're random, right?"

"Well, yeah, but..." Devon itched his arm, and I glanced down at the red marks imprinted on the inside of his elbow. "I just thought you might know, since you're tight with the coaches, and all." He looked down at his feet, refusing to meet my gaze.

"Sorry, man," I said. "Don't know what to tell you."

"Well, let me know if you hear anything, alright?" Devon asked, but had disappeared into the crowd before I could respond.

Shrugging the encounter off, I refilled my cup and headed into the house, scanning over the crowd for any familiar faces. I liked parties and knew how to handle my alcohol, but scenes like that one were a bit too big for my taste. The living room was packed with people, pulsating as one, enormous body, red Solo cups in the air, drunken faces thrown back in ecstasy. At parties like that, there were no limitations, and I'd heard my fair share of stories about what can happen in that kind of setting.

Slapping hands with fellow team members as I went, I maneuvered around the main dance floor and headed for the kitchen, my growling stomach reminding me I hadn't eaten since dinner. I spied a foldout table with cubes of cheese, and was just about to make my move when a girl stepped in my path.

"Hey, you're Aaron, right?" She asked, eyeing me up and down. I spared one last longing glance at the cheese cubes before offering the girl my best smile.

"And you are?" I asked, propping my elbow up against the wall.

"Bella North. I'm on the dance troupe."

"Oh, like hip-hop?"

She grinned. "Yep." I sized her up; she had three piercings in each ear as well as a nose ring, her tattered dark hair tied back into a messy ponytail. Her nails were as black as her clothes, stark and blatant against the polished marble floors.

"That's cool," I told her, staring down at my half-empty drink.

"I hear you're pretty good at football," she noted appraisingly, leaning into my shoulder. "You know, I'm not—"

"Aaron!" Levi interrupted, leaping at us out of thin air. Bella and I sprang apart as Levi crashed into the wall behind us, giggling dizzily.

"Hey man, you all right?" I asked, concerned. Levi bobbed his head up and down, still smiling.

"There was something I wanted to – oh, yeah! Dude, you gotta come! There's this crazy chick in the... the, um... over there!" He pointed at a nearby hallway. "Let's go, man! You *have* to see this!"

I smiled apologetically at Bella, who looked crestfallen as Levi dragged me away.

"This chick is straight *wild*," Levi chuckled, leaning against the wall for support as he struggled down the hall. The further we walked, the more the music from the living room became muffled, and a new sound emerged: people shouting.

My brow furrowed as I heard the chants of something unintelligible, watching as Levi peered curiously into the nearest open door. I followed him inside, where I found a room full of teenagers, and recognized their collective voice calling out the same word over and over again.

Chug! Chug! Chug!

I slipped into the crowd as people roared with excitement, struggling to see over the massive football players gathered around the epicenter of the room. I caught a flash of green, and a wooden framing, and realized everyone's attentions were fixed on a pool table.

As I found a spot for me to stand, I glimpsed a pair of pearly-white legs wrapped in fishnet tights, kneeling heavily on the nice fabric as the figure raised their arms above their head. I saw a funnel, and grimaced, wondering how people could urge on such animalistic behavior.

The crowd parted for a brief moment, and my heart stopped in my chest.

There, amidst a flurry of wild purple hair, was Taylor.

eyes

"What were you thinking?!" I demanded, tugging on Taylor's arm. We were stumbling across the lawn towards my car, Taylor relying heavily on me to keep her upright. "You could have gotten alcohol poisoning! There were *multiple* empty bottles, Taylor! *Multiple!*"

"A-Aaron," she slurred, pushing her purple hair out of her face.

"You turned seventeen, what, a *month* ago?!" I demanded, opening the passenger door for her to slide in. "You shouldn't be drinking that heavily, especially not in front of a whole crowd of people! I saw guys looking up your *skirt*! Jesus, your *skirt*!"

"Aaron, please take me home," she peeped, curling up into a ball as I strapped myself into the driver's seat. "I'm drunk, and I want to go home."

I sighed angrily, running my hands through my hair. "I'm not trying to be a buzzkill, it's just that..." I trailed off, gripping the steering wheel with white knuckles. "Why didn't you tell me you were coming here? I could have gone with you. How did you plan to get home? What did you—"

"Aaron, please," Taylor murmured. "I'm so... I'm so sad right now."

I swallowed, trying to compose myself. "Are you okay?" I asked in the gentlest tone I could muster up.

"I want to sleep," she mumbled, hugging her arms around her. "Sleep."

After a silent pause, I turned the key in the ignition and started the car, pulling out of the driveway to leave the flashing neon lights of the party behind us. Thankfully, I hadn't had enough to drink to be a danger on the road, and my anger substantially sobered me.

"Just... why, Taylor?" I sighed, calmer now. I was more exhausted than anything.

"I didn't want you to find out," she whispered, so softly I couldn't hear.

"What was that?" I asked.

"I didn't want you to..." She trailed off, evidently falling asleep.

"Hey, hey, stay awake!" I barked, pushing at her shoulder. When it was clear that she'd passed out, I sighed again, focusing my energy on finding the street to her house.

When we pulled up, the house was darkened, so I assumed everyone was asleep. However, as I got out and rounded the front of the car to open the passenger door, I detected movement out of the corner of my eye. When I turned to look fully, I discovered a small figure hiding in the shadows of the porch, her hair shielding her face.

"Clara," I hissed loudly. "Clara! Can you come help me?"

Clara stood and padded across the lawn, the long skirt of her nightgown swishing quietly with every step.

I reached into the car and wrapped my arm around Taylor's body, grunting as I hoisted her up into my arms.

"Get the door, will you?" I breathed, my fingernails digging into Taylor's soft skin as I carried her up the sidewalk. Clara hurried ahead and held the door open, hanging her head low so I couldn't see her face. I stepped into the darkened entryway, searching for a place to put Taylor down. "Shut it quietly, or you'll wake your parents up."

"Over there," Clara whispered, and I glanced over to see her ghostly finger pointing at a room to my right. As my eyes adjusted to the blackness, I made out the darkened form of a couch.

I set Taylor down onto the soft leather, breathing heavily as the strain was released from my shoulders. I rolled my neck and stretched my arms, easing out the tension in my muscles.

When I turned around, Clara was walking towards me with a folded blanket clutched to her chest, her feet silent on the carpet. She stepped past me without looking in my direction and draped the blanket over Taylor's still form, tucking her in tightly with the folds.

"Keep her on her side, or she could–"

"I'll stay with her," Clara whispered, still keeping her gaze on the floor as she leaned to switch on a nearby lamp. "You can go."

I licked my dry lips. After a moment, I said, "I didn't know she'd be there."

Clara stayed quiet, settling down into an easy chair near the couch, then folding her arms in her lap the same way she'd done at our tutoring session at the park.

"I would have stopped her from–"

"I know," Clara interrupted, and, for the first time since I'd known her, raised up her eyes, which were wide and bright in the dim light of the lamp. I discovered that her eyes were the most brilliant shade of blue I'd ever seen, their glistening pools piercing right through where I was standing. Taylor and the rest of her family had brown eyes, so I wondered where such a magnificent shade could have come from. A grandparent, probably.

"Right, well..." I began, backing towards the door.

"You've been drinking, too," Clara observed, still staring unblinkingly at me with her unnervingly intense eyes. "I can drive you home."

"No, really, I'm fine, I only—"

"Let me get my jacket." She finally dropped her face again, rising up from her chair to circle around me towards the coatrack. She pulled a long, gray hoodie over her nightgown, flipping her hair out and smoothing it down afterwards.

I realized that I'd never really thought about Clara driving as we headed out onto the porch. She'd been right; I did perceive her as a *little* sister, younger than her years.

Clara circled around my car and slid into the driver's side, scooting the seat way up in order to reach the pedals. As she checked the mirrors, she said, "Taylor left her car at the party." It was more of a statement than a question, but I verified it for her, anyway.

"Yeah," I told her, settling back into my seat. I realized I had a throbbing headache. Looking over at Clara, I watched her put the car into drive and speed off down the road, and I finally began to see her as a young adult, someone I could talk to the same way I talked to Taylor. "She was drinking *so much*."

Clara stayed quiet.

"I just... when I saw her *there*, in *those* tights, surrounded by *those* people..." I bit down on my lower lip to keep it from trembling.

"Aaron," Clara murmured, her voice barely louder than the car's engine.

"Yeah?" I asked, but she said all she needed to when she reached over and put her hand on my arm, stroking my bicep with her long, careful fingers.

We spent the rest of the car ride in silence, and, for once, I was glad.

girlfriend

The following morning, I woke up to an empty house, and a throbbing hangover.

As I sat up in bed, pinching the bridge of my nose between my thumb and forefinger, I recounted the previous night's events, grimacing as I remembered the sight of Taylor on the pool table. I hadn't drank a lot, but my headache was worsened by my plaguing thoughts.

I began to feel a bit stupid to have had Taylor's sister come to the rescue, then remembered that Clara wasn't just any sibling – she had acted more mature than even I had under the circumstances, remaining calm and level-headed throughout the entire ordeal. I remembered the way her eyes looked in the lamplight, glistening raw with concern and emotion, but not for her sister, for *me.*

God, it had all been a disaster.

As I went through the day, sleepwalking around like a zombie, I must have picked my phone up a dozen times. I thought about calling Taylor, but, every time I went to punch in her number, I found I couldn't bring myself to hit the dial.

I was dozing on the couch, flipping through mindless channels on TV, when a knock sounded from the doorway at around 7 PM. I was thinking about the football practice I was missing somewhere in the back of my mind, preoccupied with my sluggish brain as I padded over to the door.

And there she was, holding a bouquet of daisies as she stared up at me with huge, saddened eyes, her purple hair dancing with the chilly wind.

"Hi," Taylor said, and I was suddenly very aware that I was dressed in nothing but a tank top, shorts, and socks, my greasy hair unwashed and messy. "Can I come in?"

"Of course," I told her, stepping aside.

***

"So this is your house," Taylor murmured, gazing around the living room.

"Yeah, it's dirty right now, but both my parents have the night shift at the hospital, so I've got the place to myself." I folded my arms across my chest, watching Taylor run her fingers over the picture frames on the wall beneath the TV. "What're you standing around for? Take off your coat, kick off your shoes. You look stiff with all your gear on like that."

Taylor didn't laugh, instead fixing her lips into a tight line as she set the daisies down onto the table before silently slipping out of her jean jacket.

I plopped down on the couch, deciding I was too tired to care about how disheveled I looked.

"This is me being apologetic," Taylor said, and I looked over to see her sitting cross-legged on the couch, her hands in her lap.

"You're doing a good job," I teased halfheartedly, running my hands through my hair.

"I wanted to say I'm sorry for last night," she said, looking down at her hands. "And thanks for driving me home."

"No problem. I'm just glad we made it there in one piece; I didn't realize how trashed I was."

"Clara took the bus home."

My heart leapt in my chest, and I swallowed. "Tell her I'm sorry for that," I mumbled, folding my arms across my chest.

"And I've got some explaining to do," Taylor admitted, tucking a strand of hair behind her ear. "I'm sure you've got questions."

"Well, yeah," I said. "I mean, not really *questions*, it was just surprising to see you like... that. Completely different from how you are now, anyway."

"How I am with you," Taylor whispered beneath her breath, then looked up to meet my gaze. "It won't happen again. Next time I'm thinking of going to a party, I'll be sure to call you. And same goes for you, too, by the way."

"*I'm* not the one who can't handle my alcohol," I joked, but Taylor immediately looked hurt. "I'm sorry, that was mean." I turned to face her fully. "It's just... I don't want guys looking up your skirt."

Taylor arched an eyebrow. "I don't want that, either."

"No, I mean..." I chewed on my nail, glancing away for a moment. "I don't want *any* guys around you, looking up your skirt or not."

Taylor sat back, an amused smile playing on her lips. "Aaron Parker, are you asking me to be your girlfriend?"

"I believe I am, Taylor Lawson." I leaned forward, glancing at her lips. "No more secrets, all right?"

"All right," she agreed, and grinned.

touch

Being Taylor Lawson's boyfriend was incredible.

The first time we kissed, it felt like a fireworks show going off in my mouth, warm and powerful and new and just so *right*.

I took her to the movies, and the park, and even switched my school schedule around so we'd have the same lunch period together. Every time we were in public, I'd have my arm around her shoulders, and she'd lean into my chest, the position becoming such a common occurrence that, when I tried to hold her hand once, she'd glared at me and demanded, "the fuck do you think you're doing?" before lifting my arm and wrapping it around her neck.

I learned that her favorite food was spaghetti without meatballs, she liked dolphins and was a devoted Texas Rangers fan. I also learned other things, too; things she didn't tell me directly, but I still picked up on, anyway.

For example, I learned about the way she wrinkled her nose a bit every time she saw something she liked, and the way she unintentionally wore the same white beanie every day as soon as the cold began to really set in. The inside was practically painted purple by the time she finally got around to washing it.

I didn't go back to her house, but I did see Clara, whether it be pickups from the park or chance encounters at school. We continued our tutoring sessions on the weekends, but, when she hadn't improved after a few weeks, I decided to approach a new strategy.

"You know the material just fine," I told Clara, hugging my jacket around me as I examined her test grade. "Your grade's so low because you haven't turned in any homework. We've done, like, half of that together, so I'm just wondering how those assignments could have gotten lost between this bench and the school."

Clara hung her head low, saying nothing.

"Is it an organizational issue?"

Silence.

"Fine, then. I can wait until you decide to talk to me." I huffed in frustration, pulling my hood up over my head. "You know, for someone so adamant against being talked down to, you sure aren't helping your case by giving me the silent treatm—"

"Hot chocolate," Clara murmured, her words almost lost to the wind.

"Huh?" I asked, leaning in so I could hear her better.

"I said, let's go get some hot chocolate." Her eyes flickered up from beneath her hood. "My brain is frozen. I can't think."

I sat back. Whenever Clara talked, she always seemed to surprise me. "All right," I conceded. "But only because my ass is about to fuse together with this bench. Now, come on, hop off. Where do you want to go?"

Clara climbed off of the bench and picked her bag up from the ground. "There's a place down the road. Follow me."

We walked in silence as the wind began to pick up, desperately hugging our coats around us.

"Hey, you look cold," I told her, my teeth chattering. "You only wore a hoodie."

"Not my smartest decision," Clara admitted, her eyes fixed on the ground.

"You can take my jacket if you'd like."

"No, that's—"

"Really, if there's a place, why don't you just—" I unzipped my coat and started towards her, holding the jacket out in front of me.

"It's fine," Clara said, looking up to scan around the empty road. "Let's just—"

As soon as I draped the jacket around her shoulders, she screamed.

And *loud*.

So loud, I almost stumbled and fell, my ears ringing with the piercing shriek that had so violently ripped out of her small form. *Clara*, the one who never talked above a whisper. *Clara*, the one who spoke in short bursts, like a robot. *Clara*, the one who walked on eggshells everywhere, never daring to cross the street without an instruction manual.

Clara screamed once more, stumbling out into the open road. I watched, stunned, as her hood came down and her hair whipped around with the wind, her blue, blue eyes darting around in panic. After a moment, they landed on me, such intensity and such ferocity seared into them that I actually took a few steps back.

"Don't *touch* me!" She shrieked, and then ran.

I was frozen, watching her go. A fog had settled in, and swallowed her form up completely. It was only when she was gone that I snapped into action, pulling out my phone to dial Taylor.

She answered on the first ring. "Hey, Taylor?" I asked, out of breath. "I have a problem."

***

Taylor and I found Clara in a coffee shop down the road, sitting with her back to the door as we walked in. Her hood was pulled back up, and she sat with a steaming cup of hot chocolate in front of her, but didn't seem to be drinking it.

"Clara!" Taylor cried, maneuvering through the tables with her eyes fixed on her younger sister. "*Clara.*" She knelt down to look up into her sister's face, then began speaking in a hushed whisper, her tone grave and serious.

I lingered by the door for a moment before heading to the counter to get Taylor and myself some coffee, which the cashier handed to me right as Taylor walked up.

"She wants to be alone," Taylor told me, her eyes searching my face. "She also wants to discontinue your tutoring sessions."

I frowned. "I just wish I knew—"

"I think we should go." Taylor dropped her gaze, hugging her arms around her.

"Hey, hey," I said softly, handing her the coffee. "Shouldn't you at least stay? I can take the truck back and pick you both up later."

"No, we should just... let's go." She linked her arm through mine and tugged me towards the door, glancing over her shoulder pleadingly.

I looked at Clara one last time before following Taylor outside, my thoughts thick with confusion.

"What's up?" I asked Taylor, watching as she began to stride down the road. She said nothing, and I caught up with her, draping my arm around her shoulders. I sighed with happiness as she leaned into me, her expression unreadable.

"Clara just... she gets angry," Taylor said vaguely. "She says things she doesn't really mean."

"What did she say to you?" I asked gently, taking her hand and rubbing her shoulder.

"It's nothing." Taylor forced out a small smile for my benefit, then pointed down the road. "I'm parked over there. We can come back and get your car later. Let's go."

fight

During the days following my last session with Clara, Taylor smiled less.

I noticed that she didn't laugh at my jokes like she usually did, and often caught her staring off into the distance, her brows drawn together. She even showed up ten minutes late to the ice cream shop one afternoon, but I decided not to comment on it, out of respect for her.

I was walking her home one night when she finally broke her silence.

"Let's go to a party," she said.

My eyebrows flew up. "What?" I asked incredulously.

"A party. I want to go to a party." She bit her lip, glancing around as if a party would magically pop up out of the bushes. "You have people. Do you know if anything's going on tonight?"

"Tonight, wh–" I stepped around Taylor and tilted her chin up. "Tonight's a school night, Taylor. I don't think it's a good idea."

"What are you, my mom?" Taylor joked halfheartedly, the jab softened by a nervous laugh. As she turned to walk down the sidewalk I opened my mouth, then closed it again. "It'll be fun," she urged. "Come on, check your phone."

"Taylor..."

"Aaron."

"Won't your parents be worried?"

"They never are."

This was new. We'd never really talked about either of our family lives, except for me explaining the busy schedules of my surgeon parents, and why they thought making me get a job and share my mom's car would build character. "Taylor, let's just get you home. Take a big, warm bubble bath, and then call me. We can talk all night. All right?"

"I guess," Taylor grumbled. We fell quiet, and I chewed on my lower lip.

"Why do you want to go to a party, anyway?" I asked.

"Because they're fun."

"Well, that's a given, but they're all the same." I brushed a stray hair out of her face, then dropped my arm to rub small circles into her back. "Nothing new ever happens."

Taylor said nothing, and stayed quiet all the way back to her house, where I waited on the porch for her to unlock the front door.

"No sneaking out, okay?" I told her jokingly. "Bubble bath. Go."

"Night," she said, glancing at me briefly.

"Night," I said, watching as she disappeared into the house and slammed the door shut behind her.

I walked home, looked up at the stars, and wondered.

***

From Taylor, 12:43 AM: I'm going to a party.

***

The house was small.

Only a story high, the lawn was half-dead and scratchy, biting at my ankles as I trudged towards the front door. I glanced around nervously at the kids loitering around the entrance; they definitely weren't from the school Taylor and I went to.

Taylor. How could she do this, dragging me out of bed in the dead of night when there was school the next day?

She must be out of her mind, I thought angrily, peering at the main dance floor to try and spot her purple locks. I finally found her near the beer keg, laughing loudly with a girl that had a sleeve of tattoos on her arm.

"Taylor," I growled as I approached, upsizing the girl she was with.

"Oh, Aaron," Taylor said, and I scowled.

"You're *surprised* to see me?"

"Well... yeah." She turned to face me fully, causing the other girl to drift away behind her. "You didn't have to come. You told me to tell you if I ever went to another party, and I did."

"After what happened last time, you honestly think..." I ran my hands through my hair, tugging violently at the strands. "Is the cheap beer really worth it?"

"It's killer," Taylor told me, apparently not sensing my sarcastic tone. "You'd love it. Here, just let me pour you a cup—"

"I don't *want* a cup!" Before I knew what was happening, my arm had lashed out and knocked her drink to the floor, spattering across the worn wooden floorboards as a dark stain.

Taylor's mouth dropped open in shock, and people around us turned to look.

"Hey, this guy bothering you?" A large dude with gauges demanded, stepping towards us. "I oughta punch him good for spillin' yer drink like that."

"We're fine," Taylor murmured. She brushed past me and hooked her fingers in mine, leading me towards the front door. I eyed the big guy one last time before following her, swallowing hard to try and quell the rage bubbling up in my throat.

Taylor hurried out onto the lawn, hugging her arms around her.

"Hey, wait," I demanded, jogging to catch up. "Get in my car. I'm taking you home."

"I'm fine to drive, Aaron," Taylor said tiredly, heading towards the driver's side of her white truck.

"I'd never forgive myself if I found you wrapped around a tree tomorrow. Now, come on. I'll come back for the truck."

"Aaron, I said I'm *fine*," she snapped, sneering at me over the hood of her car. "And you know what else? I didn't *need* you to come. I don't *need* my big, strong boyfriend looking over my shoulder all the time like some goddamn parent."

53

With that, she climbed into the truck, started the engine, and drove away.

meiosis

I had a cold.

I rarely got sick, but when I did, it was the mind-numbing, feet-swelling, bedridden type.

My teammates blew up my phone for missing practice, but I was too weak to even check my messages. To make matters worse, my parents had to work, so I was left to fend for myself the entire day.

Also, Taylor didn't call.

I hadn't heard a word from her since our fight at the party. I knew I was in the right, but that didn't stop me from doubting myself. After all, I *was* the asshole that had slapped the cup out of her hands, and for that, I felt unimaginably guilty.

So I called her.

"Hey, it's me. Let's talk soon—" I sniffed, "—I'm pretty under the weather, so I'll be here all day. Call me... call me back. Okay, bye."

I hung up, groaning. Taylor Lawson had to be the most frustrating person I had ever known, and yet, I couldn't get enough of her.

I also knew she was hiding something.

It was clear enough. Besides Clara's 'thing', it was obvious she'd had other intentions when she went out to that party.

It might just have been to let off some steam, I reasoned, settling down on the couch in the living room. *After the Clara incident, I'm sure she just wanted to have some fun.*

I rubbed my face with my hands, reaching for the box of tissues.

And you ruined it for her. Asshole.

My intentions were good, but it was clear that Taylor Lawson had very different coping methods than me, methods I needed to learn to respect, and fast. My phone was quiet all afternoon, its silence ringing louder and louder with each minute that passed.

When a knock came at the door, I leapt for the knob so fast I tripped and collapsed on the floor. After I'd righted myself, I smoothed down the front of my shirt and flung the door open, ready to welcome Taylor back with open arms.

But it wasn't Taylor on my front porch.

It was Clara.

"Can I come in?" Clara asked, her eyes fixed on my chest. I took a second to process the heartbreak hammering at my ribcage before nodding silently and stepping aside.

The small girl untangled herself from her scarf, then set it down on the coffee table, taking off her messenger bag as she took my place on the couch.

"What's up?" I asked casually, sitting down beside her.

"I'm having trouble with meiosis."

My head snapped up. "Meiosis?" I echoed in disbelief.

"Yeah. Cell division. We're supposed to memorize all the stages, and I made flashcards like you said to, but I keep getting it mixed up." She stared down at her open backpack, her brow furrowed. "I was hoping you could help me."

Again, Clara had knocked me into stunned silence. "Oh, yeah. Y-Yeah. Let me just grab my laptop–" I left the room, searching around the piles of clothes littered around the hallway. "Does Taylor know you're here?" I called, grabbing my laptop off of the desk chair in my room.

"I haven't seen Taylor," Clara replied casually, sifting through some papers in her lap.

"You haven't seen her?"

"Not for a day or so." Clara looked up at me, her blue eyes shining in the light of the muted TV.

"She didn't... She didn't come home?"

"She didn't crash her car or anything, if that's what you're thinking," Clara assured me, and that, in fact, had been exactly what I was thinking. "Look, Aaron, Taylor wouldn't want me saying this, but..." She lowered her eyes, biting on her lower lip, "she isn't who you think she is. I don't know what she's got going on with you, but you were bound to find out sooner or later."

"Find out what, exactly?" I demanded, clenching my fists at my side.

"Taylor leads a double life. A lot of bad shit goes on when she stays out, and sometimes she doesn't come back for weeks."

Weeks.

"She's been staying home a lot more lately. Being nice to our parents, all that. I think you're inspiring her to be a better person."

Better person.

"So... meiosis?"

***

After I'd finished up with a brief lesson in biology, Clara and I fell into silence as we watched TV, each of us preoccupied with our own thoughts. After all the drama with Taylor, it was nice to have a few moments of peace for a little while.

"You didn't really come over for help with biology, did you?" I asked, keeping my eyes ahead as Clara sat up straighter.

"No, I didn't," she admitted. "Well, partially. I also came here to apologize for freaking out the last time we saw each other."

"That's okay," I murmured. "I just wish I'd known what it was about."

"Taylor told you not to ask, right?"

"Yeah."

She was silent, and, for a moment, I thought she would finally tell me what she had gone through.

"Anyway," she said instead, "I wanted to keep you company. I know you must be going crazy without Taylor."

I swallowed. She was exactly right, as she was proving to be more often than not. "Thank you," I said quietly.

"Want me to make you some soup?" Clara asked, standing up and brushing off her leggings. "I've got this great recipe that's perfect for treating colds."

"We have canned chicken noodle in the pantry."

"That's not as good." She headed into the kitchen, and I heard the refrigerator door open. "I'm going to make a quick grocery run. You'll be all right by yourself?" She reappeared in the living room, grabbing her scarf and bag from the couch I was sitting on.

"I'll be fine," I told her, smiling softly.

"Be right back," Clara murmured, shutting the door behind her.

soup

Clara returned an hour later, her arms full of overflowing grocery bags. I rose from the couch to help her.

"No, you sit," she ordered through the car keys in her mouth. "Stay right there. I just need a second."

I began to protest, watching her small arms struggle with the load, but eventually resigned to her stubbornness. As soon as it was clear she'd manage, I slowly sat back down onto the couch, trying to focus my attention back on the TV.

Every once in a while, I heard a crash or a bang coming from the kitchen, and couldn't help but worry. Someone of Clara's size could get trapped beneath a large pot. Maybe that was hyperbole, but I still worried.

It took Clara another hour to make the soup, broken up into twenty-minute intervals in which she brought me samples.

"Mm, it's good," I told her appraisingly, setting my cup down onto the coffee table. "You should have some."

"Oh, no," Clara said, lowering her gaze to the floor. "You can just pay me back for the groceries later."

"Aw, come on," I joked, keeling over and coughing into a tissue. "It sounds like you're cooking for an army in there. Pour yourself a cup."

Clara rubbed her arm nervously, deliberating. "*After* it's done," she finally conceded. I smiled as she turned on her heels and disappeared back into the kitchen.

Ten minutes later, she reappeared with two steaming bowls of soup on a tray, complete with glasses of water and toasted bread.

"And don't get any ideas about me being a cook," Clara told me, setting the tray down onto the coffee table. "I know how to make exactly three things: eggs, ramen, and this."

"*This* is excellent, so I can only imagine how your eggs and ramen are."

She smiled, anxiously hugging her arms around her as I dipped into the soup.

I popped the spoonful into my mouth, savoring the taste of chicken on my tongue. Clara had made the soup perfectly balanced between watery and chunky, with just the right amount of chicken and vegetables to break the broth up.

"This is a work of art," I praised, impressed with her skill.

"Dip the toast in it, too. It'll give it a little crunch."

I obeyed. "*Wow.*"

She grinned softly, reaching for the other bowl as she curled her legs up beneath her.

"Quick," I cried, causing her to startle, nearly spilling the soup on herself. "What comes after metaphase?!"

"Anaphase!" Clara answered, instantly diving into the game.

"After anaphase?"

"Telophase!"

"Very good," I said, sitting back with an easy smile. "Now, how many individual cells are produced after the end of Meiosis II?"

"Four," Clara murmured, swirling her spoon around in her bowl.

I wrinkled my nose, studying her. "You didn't need any help at all."

"That's because we've been practicing for hours."

"Yeah, but you were faking, right?" I stretched my arm along the top of the couch, glancing away. "I just don't get it, Clara. You're smart, but your grades are more tanked than an aquarium. Why don't you try in school?"

Clara was silent, hiding behind her hair, and, for a minute, I feared I'd lost her.

"I don't go to class," she finally whispered.

I stared at her. "You don't... you don't go to class?"

"No." Clara tucked her hair behind her ear, her mouth forming a tight line. "I mean, I know I should, and I hate getting yelled at, but it's not my fault."

"What do you mean?"

Clara reached beneath the coffee table and pulled out her hardcover notebook, the one I'd seen her writing in the first day at the park.

"A few years ago," she began, running her fingers lovingly over the worn spine, "I started writing down these ideas in class, but I got so absorbed in them I ended up getting humiliated whenever the teachers called on me. You know, 'cause I wasn't paying attention. So I... I just stopped going. Whenever I feel like writing, I find a spot and write. The after school detentions are helpful, too – I do the tests I missed, and I write, and nobody's allowed to talk."

I was quiet for a moment, then asked: "What do you write about?"

I caught the ghost of a smile on Clara's lips.

"*Everything*," she breathed.

***

"Thanks again for coming," I said to Clara, leaning down to peer at her through the open driver's window. She'd taken her parents' car to come see me, since Taylor's truck was still missing, along with Taylor. "Hope I didn't get you sick."

"Nah, I've got a good immune system," she assured me, leaning to turn the key in the ignition. "I'll call you when Taylor gets home."

My heart leapt up into my throat. "Thank you," I murmured, stepping away as she rolled up the window.

I backed away from the truck as the engine revved to life, standing in the middle of the empty road as I watched Clara speed off into the night. It was late, and I was going to try to go to school the next morning, so I knew I had to get to bed.

I trudged towards the house, my hands in my pockets, reviewing all of the conversations Clara Lawson and I had had over the past afternoon.

Taylor's little sister was proving to be just as interesting as she was.

coffee

The next morning, Taylor texted me.

I was getting ready for school, pulling on my clothes as I stepped out of a steamy shower, and eyed my phone's screen where it was glowing on my nightstand. After taking my time to comb my hair and slap on some cologne, I casually sauntered over and checked my texts, unsurprised when Taylor's name popped up.

I also wasn't as surprised as I should have been as I stared down at those two words:

I'm sorry.

We decided to meet before school for coffee, so I pulled up to her house in my mom's car, blinking as I watched her climb into the passenger's seat. She looked frazzled – her hair was tied up into two messy buns, and bags underneath her eyes stretched down lower than I'd ever seen them before.

We drove to a place near the campus called *Auntie Veronica's*, remaining silent throughout the entire drive.

As soon as I parked, however, I'd barely had time to unbuckle my seatbelt before Taylor had rounded the car, thrown her arms around me, and dragged me out onto the sidewalk.

"*I'm sorry*," she wept, her voice breaking as she buried her face into my shoulder.

Suddenly, with that one gesture, that one embrace, all my tension melted away, and I found myself hugging her back, breathing in the sweet scent of her purple hair.

"It's okay," I murmured, stroking the back of her head. "Don't cry. It's okay."

I looked around, my eyes landing on a couple eating outside (God knows why, it was practically subarctic) as they glanced curiously in our direction. I managed to detangle myself from Taylor and walk her into the shop, my arm around her shoulders as she pulled out her pocket mirror.

"My mascara's all smudged," she sniffed, dabbing at the affected area with some concealer. "Thank goodness I didn't get anything on your shirt. God, I'm a mess."

"No, you're not," I told her, pulling out a chair at a nearby table. "Stay here. I'll grab some coffee."

"Black, please."

"Gotcha." When I'd returned with our drinks, Taylor sipped hers silently, her shoulders hiked up to her ears. "Where were you yesterday?" I asked casually, attempting to be gentle, so as not to upset her.

"I took a drive," Taylor said, twirling a strand of violet hair around her finger. "I just got in my car, and drove. It's a good thing I did, too, because I *really* needed to clear my head." She raised her big, brown eyes to mine, her bottom lip quivering. "Just know... it wasn't me. The girl that went to that party without your permission—"

"You don't need my permission to go to a party. I just worry about you."

"Well, you shouldn't." She shook her head adamantly. "I don't know, I was upset, and I – I'm not reckless. I promise."

"I don't think you are." I smiled kindly at her over the rim of my cup. "Don't stress, okay? Today's gonna be fun."

"Yeah." She sat back, breathing out a sigh of relief. "It will be. Just don't expect to ever see that Taylor again, because that Taylor wasn't me."

As I sipped my coffee, I couldn't help but remember Clara's haunting words:

She isn't who you think she is.

***

The next day was football practice, one the last ones before the first game of the season.

Could u stay after school? I texted Taylor as I sat in the library. *Id rly love if u could come to my practice.*

Why's that?

Because, #1, ur my gf & I want 2 show u off, & #2, I'm freezing my ass out there for 3 hours, u might as well keep me company.

Hmm

U don't have to stay 4 the whole thing. What do u say?

I cant make today

My heart sank. *Why not?*

Clara issues

What about her?

Idk the exact details, but mom needs me home right after school

:(

Tell u what, I can come to the homecoming game. It's next Friday, right?

Yea

I can def come to that!! Are u mad?

No, never

Gr8! I'll text u later :)

Can't wait! Byeeee

I shut off my phone and sat back against my chair, picturing Taylor's smiling face cheering me on from the stands.

It was almost too good to be true.

doorbell

The next day was Saturday, and my parents were home.

"Morning, honey," Mom cooed as she staggered into the kitchen, dressed in a pink bathrobe and slippers. "God, I pulled a 48-hour shift. You have no idea how good decent sleep felt."

"I can only imagine," I sympathized, gesturing with my mug at the coffee I'd brewed. "Dad's home, too?"

"Yep. Finally, a slow weekend." She checked her pager as she poured herself some coffee, a habit I'd come to expect from her. "I'd whip up some breakfast, but I'm a little sluggish right now."

"That's okay. I already ate."

"You did?"

"Yeah. Eggs." I nodded my head at the sink, where the pan I'd used was waiting to be washed.

"Oh, wow, it's 10:50," mom noted, staring at the clock on the microwave. "I guess brunch for me, then."

"Is it cool if I go over to Taylor's this afternoon?"

Mom's brow furrowed. "Who's Taylor?"

I blinked. "My girlfriend."

An awkward pause passed. "Why didn't you–"

"I talk about her all the time, mom."

"Oh, wow. Brain fart. I guess I've never met her though, right?"

"No."

"Well, then. What's she like?"

"She has purple hair."

"The eccentric type. I like her already." Mom's eyes shined with pride, thinly veiled over her obvious exhaustion. "Let's have her over for dinner sometime."

"She's coming to the first game. I was thinking I could bring her to the cookout."

"Sounds good. So, this afternoon?"

"Yeah, you and dad can carpool to work like usual, right?"

Mom pursed her lips. "We're staying home today. We're here."

Dad poked his head into the kitchen. "Hello, family!" He chirped, his usual greeting. "Anything to eat?"

"Grab yourself some toast," mom told him. "Let's sit down and have a civilized meal for once, shall we?"

I heard a beep, and didn't have to look up to recognize the distinct sound of dad's pager. "Oh, honey..." He began.

"*No*," mom moaned, slumping against the counter. "We've worked, what? Eighty hours this week? It's time for a break, Scott. Let someone else take it."

"They need us, sweetie," dad reminded her. "I'm just as unhappy about it as you are, but a trauma's coming in hot. Car wreck, six injured."

Mom rested her forehead against the cabinet. "*No.*"

"Honey..."

"Fine. Go get dressed. I'll meet you in the car."

Dad nodded and left, leaving my mother and I alone in the kitchen.

"So, you guys won't be here this afternoon?" I asked, and mom stiffened.

She left the room quietly.

***

"What happened with Clara?" I asked Taylor as we lounged on her bed, a photo album open on my lap. She'd requested that I bring it over.

"Something to do with the *incident*," Taylor said vaguely, and I wrinkled my nose at her.

"Shut up and just tell me what happened already."

"I like driving you crazy." She looked up and smiled at me. "I also need a copy of this picture of you in the pool. Look at your little butt!" She pointed at the page, where I met eyes with a smiling three-year-old me.

"Give me that," I laughed. "Don't you have enough blackmail on me already?"

"What, like your hourly updates on the zit on your chin?"

"You *wanted* those. It's all out of context! I will not be threatened!"

She laughed, falling into my chest with shaking shoulders. I tackled her onto the bed, the album sliding onto the floor, and kissed around her jawline, the scent of her filling my lungs.

Soon, we had escalated into a hot make-out session, my hands roaming around her hips and lower back, pulling her closer and closer to me, unable to get enough of her. Taylor's fingers combed through my hair, her lips traveling over mine as one everlasting, breathless kiss.

Then the doorbell rang.

The mood shattered into a million pieces, and I groaned as Taylor pulled away from me, raising her head to look at the closed bedroom door.

"Stay," I groaned, tugging her back down. "It's probably just the mail guy, or something."

"Yeah, my–" The doorbell rang again, echoing eerily throughout the silent house. "I'll be right back."

"Noo," I sighed, flopping back against the bed as I grabbed onto her hands.

"One second! Just one second!" She smiled as she detangled herself from me before hopping off the bed, smoothing down her shirt, and heading for the door. I laid back as I listened to her footsteps quietly pad downstairs, my eyes finding the framed pictures on top of Taylor's dresser.

I swung my legs over the side of the bed and headed across the room, smiling at the pictures of young Taylor laughing and playing. Her hair was strawberry blonde, bright and vibrant in comparison to Clara's light brown locks. Clara was in many of those pictures, too – she seemed a lot happier and healthier than she was as a teenager.

Realizing Taylor had been gone for a little while, I stepped towards the door and heard the sound of voices talking quietly in the entryway. I headed out into the hallway and paused at the top of the stairs.

"You need to leave. *Now*," Taylor's stern voice said, and my brow furrowed.

"C'mon, man," a guy's nervous voice peeped. "I just need some–"

"I don't *care* what you need," Taylor barked. "You *never* come here. You understand me? God, I can't believe–"

"Jeffery vouched for you! I thought you'd be–"

"Did Jeffery give you this address?"

"No, I looked you up."

"Fuck. Just... just... go. Right now."

"Fine, whatever."

I'd just started down the stairs when I stopped, realizing Taylor still hadn't closed the door.

"Are you going straight, or something?" The guy's voice asked. "'Cause if you are, I gotta let my guys know—"

"Just *leave*. I'll be in touch, but if you *ever* come here again, I'll beat your ass senseless. Got it?"

Taylor slammed the door shut, turning on her heels in a huff. As she headed up the stairs, she looked up to see where I was standing, and her mouth dropped open in surprise.

"I—" she began, blinking rapidly. "That was—"

I stayed silent, watching as she hugged her arms around her and tucked her hair behind her ears.

I stepped down a stair, but she held her hand up to stop me.

"We agreed no more secrets," she began softly. "I think we need to have a talk."

park

I was sitting in my car later that night, absentmindedly staring out through the dark windshield.

Taylor and I had talked for hours; or rather, *she'd* talked, going over and over bullshit excuses that left my head spinning. By the time I left, her story had changed so many times that I wasn't sure if the guy at the door had been her ex-boyfriend or long-lost brother.

I started the engine, listening to the soft murmuring as it rumbled to life.

I knew one thing for certain; Taylor was lying to me, and I couldn't figure out why.

However, I did know someone who might have answers.

***

The next day, I found Clara at the same park she'd always been at, sitting on the same swing she'd always sat on, writing in the same blue journal she'd always been writing in. Clara was predictable, and I liked that. She was reliable that way.

I shut the door to my car and locked it, starting across the lot towards the swing set. Clara's earbuds were plugged in, so she didn't look up as I approached.

Remembering her skittishness, I reached out and gently removed one of her earbuds, pleased when she didn't scream her head off. Instead, she startled violently, her blue eyes whirling around to meet mine.

"Aaron," she breathed, not lowering her gaze.

"Hi, Clara," I said meekly. "I was hoping we could talk."

She blinked, then slowly removed her other earbud. I glanced down at the page she was writing in, but was only able to make out one word before she slammed the cover shut.

Dead.

"Should we go there?" Clara asked, tilting her head in the direction of the bench.

I nodded silently, stepping around her to head across the park with my hands in my pockets. I heard the creak of the swing set and the rustle of grass behind me as Clara followed. I didn't have to turn around to know she would be stepping lightly with her journal pressed up against her chest, just like she always did.

I turned and sat on the bench, looking up to watch Clara timidly take a seat beside me.

"Are you okay?" Clara asked, dropping her gaze.

"Yeah, I guess," I murmured, running my hands through my hair. "It's just... I was over at your house yesterday."

Clara's brow furrowed. "Did you go into my room?"

"No, no. Of course not. The door was shut, anyway."

Clara sat back, evidently relieved. "Go on, then."

"I was hanging out with Taylor, when an... *unexpected* visitor arrived."

Clara's jaw clenched, and I had a feeling she knew who I was talking about.

"I didn't get a good look at the guy, but I heard him talking to Taylor about her 'going straight'. You only go straight if you've been crooked, right?"

Clara shrugged, but I took it as confirmation.

"She talks about her past, but I have a feeling she's left out parts," I sighed, running my hands over my jeans. "And now she's lying to me, Clara. I just... I don't know what to do." I clenched my jaw. "I don't know what to do."

Clara was silent for a good minute. "You know I can't tell you anything about Taylor that she doesn't want to tell you herself, right?"

"I know," I said, nodding solemnly. "I just thought... ugh, I don't know what I thought. I'm not even sure why I'm here." I stood. "I'm sorry I interrupted you."

I'd just turned to leave when Clara reached out and put her hand on mine. "Aaron," she whispered softly, my name falling through her lips like a feather floating to the ground. Her gentleness made me pause, looking down at where her fingers were overlapping mine. "Does Taylor love you?"

I slowly sat back down. "I don't know. I think I love her, but I haven't said it yet."

"If she loves you, she trusts you," Clara told me. "It's not one before the other. It's both at the same time. If she's lying to you, she doesn't love you yet."

I felt like crying. "I don't know what else I can do."

"You've been the perfect boyfriend, Aaron. She even talks to me about how much she likes hanging out with you. If you keep doing what you're doing, she will love you, I guarantee. It just takes time. You can't rush it."

"But *I'm* ready," I murmured. "I'm ready to love her."

Clara took her hand off of mine, retracting it to place it on the journal in her lap. "Then you can wait. Right?"

I swallowed. "It's hard."

"You can only love her more and more. If you wait, she'll come to you. I promise."

I said nothing.

"I know you didn't sign up for all of this when you decided to date her," Clara told me, "but Taylor's a full package. A big, complicated package."

I couldn't help but smile. "You're not exactly black-and-white your-self."

Clara grinned, dropping her head down to her lap. "Must run in the family."

I couldn't help but laugh. Between Clara's abstruseness, Mrs. Lawson's coldness, and Mr. Lawson's out-of-place cheeriness, Clara's words were far, far too true. And there, at the heart of it all, was Taylor, the crown jewel.

Clara was right. Taylor was worth waiting for.

"Thank you," I said, holding my arms out. "Is it all right if I hug you?"

"I'm not big on the whole 'touching' thing, if you hadn't noticed."

"Just this once."

Sighing, she leaned into me as I wrapped her into my chest, pressing my cheek against her thin hair.

"Go get her," Clara whispered, and I stood up again.

movies

"Movies. Tomorrow."

"I–"

"It's not a question, Taylor. And *you're* paying for popcorn, since you get to choose the movie."

There was a pause. "I get to choose the movie?"

"That's right."

"What about *Love Dearest?*"

"Are you *serious?* That sappy chick flick?!"

"It's a work of *art*, you moron."

"I'm not paying eighteen bucks for *Love Dearest.*"

"I can pay for my ticket."

"No... dammit." I sighed. "*Love Dearest* it is. Find out the show times; I'll call you later."

"Okay. Hey, Aaron?"

"Taylor?"

"I love you."

My mouth dropped open, the wheel in my hand swerving violently. Luckily, I was driving on an empty road.

I hung up without responding.

***

Taylor didn't call again.

In fact, I was pretty sure she wouldn't ever call again. I mean, if I told a guy I loved him and he hung up on me, I probably wouldn't be in a huge rush to see him, either.

I had to get my thoughts together. Clara had said just the day before, *"if she loves you, she trusts you. It's not one before the other. It's both at the same time."* But Taylor still wasn't coming forward about lying, and yet she'd told me that she loved me.

Which meant she was lying about loving me.

I flopped back against my bed, rubbing my hands up and down my face. I felt more alienated to Taylor than I had since we'd met, like the connection between us was wearing dangerously thin. I wanted to grapple to save our relationship, but it was like I didn't have enough energy. Every lie Taylor told me – every secret she kept – felt like a punch to the face. I knew I had to confront her, one way or another.

I didn't even register the knock at my front door until I was heading down the hallway, my head hanging low. I looked like a mess – I was wearing a white tank top and gray sweatpants, and hadn't showered since the day before. I found myself not caring, too drained to do anything but pull open the door and set my sights on the girl on the porch.

"Ready to go?" Taylor asked, her smile huge. "*Love Dearest* wasn't exactly sold out, so I'm sure we can get there a little late."

I stared at her, my mouth hanging open like a fish.

"What?" Taylor asked, her brows drawing together. "Do I have something in my teeth?"

"No, uh..." I sputtered, running my hands through my hair as I took a step backwards. "It's just... come in, come in."

She obeyed, stepping over the threshold, then heading straight for the couch.

"I'll go get changed," I murmured, slipping past her and into the hallway.

***

Love Dearest actually wasn't all that bad.

I'm not a fan of those type of movies, but, with my arm around Taylor as she hand-fed me popcorn, things were feeling pretty great.

That was the effect Taylor had on me. When I was with her, I could forget she was lying, forget all of the mistakes we'd both made. I even thought at one point, *now we're even. You hung up on her, and she lied to you. Everything's fair now.*

Or maybe we were more broken than ever. I didn't know.

What I did know was that Taylor belonged at my side, nestled into the crook of my arm as her hand snaked around my waist and pulled me close. Something about her just felt so incredibly *right*, so incredibly *incredible*.

"Let's go to the mall, or something," Taylor sighed, swinging in front of me on the sidewalk so she could grab my hands. "I'm in a shopping mood."

I grinned down at her as I leaned over to let our noses touch. "My wallet, however, is not," I joked.

"Oh, hush. You know I've got cash."

"Yeah, and quite the wad of it," I recalled, remembering when she'd paid for the popcorn at the concessions stand. "How'd you get so much money, anyway?"

"Smuggling drugs across the border."

"Very noble of you."

She laughed and kissed me, her lips tasting like butter. "We can walk there, right? It's only, like, three miles."

"Now wait a–" I was interrupted by her phone ringing in her jacket, and scoffed at her. "You're supposed to *silence* it, Miss Lawson. What would have happened if that had gone off in the theater?"

"Oh, shut up," Taylor growled, playfully shouldering my chest as she pulled out her cell. "It's mom. I've gotta take this."

I groaned. "Oh, the woeful life of me."

"Hush up! Mom?" She plugged her other ear with her finger as I pulled her into my arms, nuzzling her purple hair. "Yeah, we're out. The theater on Burke Street, why?" Suddenly, she went rigid in my embrace, and I pulled back, realizing her face was grim. "Wait – mom? Slow down. Wait, I'm – no, your connection's bad. Start from the beginning."

A long stretch of silence passed.

"She... she..." Taylor began, but was cut off. I watched her mouth open and shut, her eyes flying around like bullets. "I... we'll be right there." She held the phone away from her ear, staring at it for a moment before slowly reaching up to end the call.

"What's up?" I asked, trying to be casual.

Taylor looked at me, her eyes wide with terror.

"Clara's in the hospital," she said.

hospital

I couldn't breathe.

I couldn't breathe as Taylor crushed my hand in her grip. I couldn't breathe as she tugged me, full-speed, into the ER waiting room. I couldn't breathe as I caught sight of Mrs. Lawson lying on the floor.

There was no air in the room.

"Mom!" Taylor exclaimed, throwing herself down beside the blonde-haired woman. "What happened?!"

"I... I don't know," Mrs. Lawson whispered, her eyes staring past her daughter into empty space. "I was just... giving her medicine. Every day, same dose. And then she's seizing, and bleeding, and foaming, and..." I'd never seen a woman look so vulnerable as I watched Mrs. Lawson curl in on herself, wrapping her arms around Taylor's shoulders, "the *sound*, Taylor. The sound she made..."

Both of them dissolved into fits of sobbing, and I was left standing there, feeling completely numb. Clara knew the ins and outs of Taylor and how to handle her. Clara was a key; deciphering Taylor's secrets, calming me down – she was my *friend*.

I turned around and stumbled towards the reception, gripping onto the counter like it was my lifeboat.

"I need the room number of a patient. Clara Lawson," I told the secretary.

"Are you family?" The woman asked, smacking her gum. She was *bored*. I felt enraged.

"No," I growled through my teeth.

"Then, sorry, but you can't see her. She's in critical care, anyway. Nobody's allowed in."

Critical care.

I left the counter and collapsed into a seat behind Mrs. Lawson and Taylor, who were still sitting on the floor. My thoughts were racing – so many voices were screaming at me that everything faded back into a dull roar, a hollow ringing sound taking over my mind. I leaned forward and put my head in my hands, thinking of Clara's blue, blue eyes.

She didn't deserve this.

Mr. Lawson arrived, sprinting into the ER with his shirt half-buttoned. Even *he* couldn't be cheerful during such an intense time. I watched as he picked Taylor and Mrs. Lawson off of the floor and deposited them into the seats next to me, rubbing Mrs. Lawson's shoulders soothingly.

He was being strong for them, which meant I had to be strong, too.

The next hour and a half was spent in agonizing worry, each minute that passed tripling the anxiety hanging in the air like a heavy weight. I didn't even pull out my phone – I was too busy alternating between comforting Taylor and trying to keep myself together. I'd never lost anyone. All my grandparents were still alive. If Clara were to die...

No. I refused to think about it.

"Mr. and Mrs. Lawson?" A voice asked, and my head snapped up to see a perky blonde doctor with a clipboard standing in front of us. Everyone stood, trembling visibly. "Clara is out of immediate danger."

A collective sigh of relief rose up, my shoulders sagging so heavily I had to sit back down in my chair.

"She's being transferred to the ICU," the doctor went on. "She'll remain under round-the-clock supervision for the next few days."

"D-Do you know what happened?" Mrs. Lawson blubbered, pressing a wad of tissues to her nose, and the doctor's lips tightened.

"We found a bottle containing illegal pills in Clara's bag," the doctor explained gently. "We pumped her stomach, but, because the pill contained toxic chemicals, it acted on her body in the same manner as poison would."

I sucked in a sharp breath.

"As I said, Clara is out of immediate danger, but it will take a few days to fully flush out the toxins. She's heavily sedated right now, but you can go in and see her, if you'd like."

I stood, and the doctor's eyes fell on me. "Immediate family only," she said, and my jaw tightened.

"I'll come back," Taylor told me, her voice breaking as she touched my hand. "Just... I'll come back." She hurried off after Mr. and Mrs. Lawson, leaving me in the ER waiting room, alone.

***

Taylor returned an hour later, without her parents.

"I'm going to drive you home," she murmured, pulling her car keys out of her pocket.

"How is she?" I asked softly, following her towards the exit.

"She's hooked up to all these machines," Taylor choked, hanging her head in sorrow. "She can't breathe on her own, or something. I... I feel like it's my fault."

"Why would you think that?" I asked, feeling the cold breeze blast against me as we stepped outside.

"We – never mind."

I fell behind her as we walked to her car, gritting my teeth to keep back the two words ringing out in my brain.

More lies.

writing

Two days later, Clara's health had improved, so she was moved to a regular hospital room, where I was allowed to visit her.

I lingered outside of the door for a long while, debating on how to approach the situation. Taylor wasn't with me; we hadn't spoken since our last interaction in the hospital parking lot. She needed her space, and I needed mine, but for different reasons.

I pushed the door in.

Clara glanced up from her journal, a small grin spreading across her face. "Aaron," she said happily, tucking her hair behind her ears. "What a nice surprise."

"How're you feeling?" I asked, perching on the edge of her bed.

"Hurt," Clara muttered, wincing as she pressed her fingers to her stomach. "I'm really weak, too, but I've started being able to eat again, so that's good."

"Yeah," I said softly, smoothing down the covers on the bed. I looked at her, then grinned at the pen in her hand. "You'd think you'd have filled that notebook up by now."

"Oh, I have," Clara told me, nodding enthusiastically. "I have three of these. This blue one, a yellow one, and a black one."

"Which came first?"

"The black one."

"Why'd you start writing?"

She grinned. "You're trying to get my story out of me, Aaron Parker."

I pressed my hand to my chest, mock offended. "I have no idea what you're talking about!" I gasped dramatically, batting my eyelashes. "How dare you accuse me of such a thing, Clara Lawson."

She smiled softly, looking down at her lap. "Want to read this page?"

I stopped. "Really?"

"Yeah. I mean, if you want to. I know reading isn't most people's thing, and it takes forever to—"

"Gimmie," I screeched, tugging the book away from her. "This page?"

"*Only* that page."

"It's barely half full! You're ripping me off."

"Take it or leave it."

"Fine," I grumbled, smiling. "Do you want me to read it out loud?"

"God, no."

I wrinkled my nose at her and returned my focus to the page, tracing my finger over Clara's spidery writing. She wrote in small capital letters, the exact opposite of her lowercase text talk. The page was smeared in spots where the ink hadn't had time to dry.

I began to read.

Within the waves of the cotton bedsheets, she found herself awakening in a dream-like state, the walls bending and twisting with dizziness as her eyes landed on the eggshell-colored wallpaper. Her arms were numb — they felt detached to her body entirely. She attempted, for a brief moment, to sit up, but her abdomen seized with pain, spasming dangerously. She wished

I gaped down at the page, stunned.

"What does she wish?!" I demanded, throwing the book back at Clara. "How could you do that to me?!"

"*Me*?!" Clara demanded through a fit of laughter. "*You* came in and interrupted!"

I decided I liked her laugh, but it may have been heightened by my relief to see her alive at all. Her voice floated through the air like a perfect melody.

"Well, anyway, it's *really* good," I complimented her. "No, scratch that. It's not just good, it's *incredible*."

For the first time since I'd met her, Clara Lawson actually blushed. She dropped her head and retreated into herself, but in a better way than normal. "I know you're just saying that," she peeped.

"No, I mean it, Clara. You're so talented. You ought to be; you spend 24-7 with that book."

Clara peered up, her face half-hidden by her hair. "That's from when I woke up here. Right after that, I fell unconscious again, so the doctors thought I'd woken up for the first time a few hours later. But I remember this — this one moment where I felt almost half-dead. I hope I never have to feel that again."

I frowned sympathetically, snaking my hand out to grasp hers. "Bad pills, huh?"

Clara scoffed. "I'm a dumbass. It's my own fault. I wanted..." She trailed off, lowering her eyes again. I stroked the back of her knuckle with my thumb, waiting for her to finish.

"What's up?" I asked, moving up to get a better look at her face.

"I just wanted to sleep," Clara murmured, running her free hand through her hair as she stared down into her lap. "I don't... I just wanted..." she sucked in a deep breath, composing herself. "I wanted to know what it was like to dream again."

"So why didn't you ask your parents for sleeping pills?"

"Even if they handed out the dosage, they'd think I'd try and kill myself. They... they treat me like some fragile little bird, a bomb waiting to explode. You know?" She laughed quietly. "Sorry. I don't know why I'm telling *you* this, or anyone at all, really."

"You have a lot of thoughts in your head," I told her, watching her glance shyly up at my face. "If you ever need an open ear, I'm here. All right?"

She smiled brilliantly. "All right," she said.

***

An hour later, I lingered out in the hall for a moment, my hand on the doorknob as I prepared to leave.

"Clara?" I asked, watching as she looked up from her writing.

"Yeah?" She asked, her pen poised mid-word.

"Where did you get the pills?" I asked, knowing that she wasn't sociable enough to get her hands on illegal medicine easily.

Clara was quiet, and my brow furrowed.

"Clara," I began, stepping fully into the room. "I'm not a cop. I just want to know. You've been honest with me so far; can you be honest with me now?"

Another long minute of silence passed before Clara finally nodded her head, still keeping her mouth shut.

"I'll ask again," I told her gently. "Clara, where did you get the pills?"

She tucked her hair behind her ears, her eyelashes fluttering, her shoulders hiked up to her ears. She forced herself to look up at me, a gesture that took obvious strength.

"Taylor," Clara finally said.

accelerate

When Taylor opened her front door, I was done skirting around everything. I was done pretending that we were okay, pretending that her lying to me okay, pretending that I was going to sit around and stay quiet for another single moment.

"I love you, Taylor," I said, staring right into her chocolatey brown eyes. "I love you, and you don't love me. If you loved me, you wouldn't be constantly lying to me. If you loved me, you wouldn't be treating me like this. If you loved me, you'd know I'm not a *fucking dumbass*. I see right through you – you're hiding from me, and I've done nothing but love and support you ever since the day we met. I tried being open, hoping you'd eventually come around, but I can't wait any longer. You have to choose me, Taylor. You have to choose me over whatever it is you're hiding. I promise it'll be so much better than *lying all the fucking time*."

Taylor's mouth opened, then closed. "You don't know," she murmured, dropping her eyes. "You don't understand."

"I *want* to understand. But I never will, unless you're honest with me. Right now, Taylor."

She sighed, folding her arms across her chest. "What do you want to know?"

"Well, for starters, who was that guy at the door? Why did you give your sister a bottle of illegal pills? How did you get those pills? Why can't you get along with your mom? I have *so* many questions, Taylor, but I don't want you to answer them right now. I just want you to fill in the blanks from here on out. I don't need an interrogation session, I need to go on loving you with complete and total honesty from your end. Every time you think, '*I shouldn't say this*', I want you to *say it*. Do you understand?"

"Aaron, you should respect me enough to leave me alone when I'm uncomfortable talking about something. Think of me like Clara."

I scowled. "Don't compare yourself to her. It's clear Clara's been through something traumatic, but you – you're just hiding for, what? Sport? *Nothing* on this earth will make me love you any less than I do right now. Whatever you say, it will not change my mind about how I feel about you. Not ever."

If she loves you, she trusts you. It's not one before the other. It's both at the same time.

What Clara *didn't* say was that sometimes you have to take matters into your own hands – accelerate the process before it spirals out of control.

Taylor was silent, staring up at me with huge, worried eyes.

"You could say you murdered my family and took a shit on my car and I wouldn't care," I finished.

Taylor looked over my shoulder. "Nope," she said. "All clear. The windshield, at least."

We grinned at each other. "Really," I told her. "Whenever you want to, just lay it on me. I can't possibly imagine why you'd be hesitant to tell me something, because you really, *really* shouldn't be. We're together now, Taylor. That means I'm here for you, okay?"

Taylor sagged visibly. "I can't talk to my family about anything," she whispered. "M-My friends... nobody understands me."

I stepped forward and took her into my arms. "You're speaking English, aren't you?"

She laughed through her tears.

***

"I hadn't tried the pills," Taylor whispered, pacing restlessly around the room. "My friend Rob gave them to me to help me sleep, but I thought Clara needed them more than I did, so I gave them to her. It's my fault." She laughed humorlessly. "Well, at least my relationship with my family can't get any worse, right?"

"What about your dad?" I asked, lounging on her bed. "He seems like the household peacekeeper."

"*That* man?" She scoffed, stopping to fold her arms across her chest. "*That* man is as clueless as they come. Either that, or he really wants to believe he lives in a perfect house, in a perfect neighborhood, in a perfect, perfect world. He's an optimist, or whatever. Clara was the same way."

"'Was'? You mean before the '*incident*'?"

"Yeah. Before that." She shot me a glare. "I'm Miss Honesty now, but it's actually a family rule that Clara has to tell you about that. I can't say anything."

"I didn't ask you to."

"Yeah, but you were *thinking* it."

"So I'm penalized for thinking now?"

"Exactly." She climbed onto the bed and straddled me, pieces of wispy purple hair falling loose from her bun. "I think I'm in love with you, Aaron Parker."

And this time, she meant it.

***

As I left Taylor's house, I realized we were only a few days away from the first game of the football season, and I was getting rusty. I called up Levi and some others, and had them meet me at the field.

"I like your spunk, brother!" Levi praised, slapping me on the back as I pulled on my helmet. "Surprise practices keep us on our toes."

"It's not an *official* practice," I reminded him.

"Well, yeah, but still. You've been spending so much time with that girl of yours, we barely ever see you."

I raised an eyebrow at him. "You know her?"

"Y'all eat lunch together *every day*. It's not subtle, dude."

"We're not trying to be." I grinned at him. "Her name's Taylor."

"Big tits?"

"I'm going to kick your ass."

"If it scores a touchdown, by all means, do it!"

We laughed as we jogged out onto the field, my heart fluttering all the way.

gone

Clara, 1:42 AM:

taylor's missing.

***

I could have never pictured I'd be squatting there, over an open man-hole at 2 o'clock in the morning, more scared than I'd ever been in my entire life.

"She can fit down there, right?" I demanded, pointing down into the dark abyss. "If she was drunk, she could've stumbled and fallen–"

"It's a hazard, no doubt," Clara told me, hugging her hoodie around her as she bounced up and down to keep warm. "I don't think she's in there, though."

"Why not?"

"First of all, Taylor never goes this way home. It's out of her way, and just an unnecessary road to take."

"Then why are we here, then?!" I grabbed at my hair.

"I was searching Pond Avenue when *you* called and told me to come here, remember?" She wrinkled her nose in the dim moonlight. "If you're this freaked out by a pothole, how do you think you'll be when we actually find her?"

"What does *that* mean?! I'm just confused, Clara. Confused, and tired. Is Taylor even missing at all?"

Clara frowned. "Of course she is. I wouldn't make that up. And I know I said that she goes away sometimes, but this is different. She called me."

I froze. "She called you?"

"Yes. At around 1:30."

"Why didn't you tell me? What'd she say?"

"She was nonsensical. Been out all night. I wasn't – I could barely make anything out. I did hear her say, 'I'm in trouble, boo', and she sounded scared, so I got dressed, got my parents' car, and texted you."

"That's *nothing*, Clara! We both know Taylor goes to parties, she could just be wasted out of her mind!"

"Something's wrong," Clara mumbled quietly. "She called me 'boo'. She hasn't called me that since we were little."

"That doesn't mean anything."

"Look, Aaron, I *know* Taylor, and I think she's in trouble, so I need your help."

I clenched my jaw.

"If you're still in denial–"

"I'm not," I interrupted. "Let's just find her." I folded my arms across my chest. "So, Pond Avenue?"

"The one with the pond."

"I could've guessed."

"Sometimes Taylor and her friends like to go swimming there. I checked all over, but I didn't see any signs that anyone had been by recently."

"Well, of course not. It's freezing."

Clara was quiet, and I turned to face her fully. "What?" I asked.

"It's freezing," Clara murmured, deep in thought. "Where's someplace that's warm?"

"I don't know, the library, the school, the—"

"*Taylor's car,*" Clara whispered.

My mouth dropped open.

"Oh, no."

***

"Slow down, Paul Walker. You're going to kill us."

"Will you just let me drive?" I growled, gripping the wheel with white knuckles. "Are the blinders on? They're on, right?"

"Yes, they're on." Clara sighed. "If there's anything there, we'll see it. Stop stressing, okay?"

"I don't understand how you can be this calm. This is unusual, right?"

"Definitely worth the concern, but you have to stay level-headed. If you're panicking, you won't think clearly, and, right now, we need to think clearly."

She was absolutely right. I sat back against my seat, sucking in deep breaths of air.

"Okay, now," Clara went on. "Let's start with the park. Then we go to the ice cream shop, then to Devon's house."

My brow furrowed. "Devon?"

"Yeah, her friend. You know him, he's on the football team."

I blinked, remembering when he'd approached me at the party a few weeks ago. "Are they–"

"Taylor is many things, but she is not a cheater," Clara assured me, reaching over to steady my shaking arm. "She was cheated on when she was younger, so that's absolutely off-limits. It isn't even worth thinking about. Aaron?"

"Yeah, I hear you," I murmured, lowering my eyes. "It's just, guy friends normally–"

"*Friends* even goes a little too far. They've hung out maybe three times, and I've only seen him once. They probably just drink together, or something."

I didn't like Clara's uncertainty. I was about to question her further when she pointed out the window.

"There's the park."

We pulled into the lot, the tires crunching over loose gravel. I squinted to see through the darkness, keeping both hands on the wheel. Before I knew what was happening, Clara had unbuckled her seatbelt, and began to climb out.

"Hey, wait!" I cried. "Where are you going?"

"I'm just gonna go check it out. Keep the headlights on."

"I'm coming with you."

"You've got a hundred pounds on me, so I won't stop you."

We slammed the car doors shut and began to trek towards the swing set, the lights from the car casting shadows of us on the ground. Beside the swings was a jungle gym and a sand pit, a small setup completely surrounded by a large field that stretched out until it hit the edge of a forest.

"Are we sure we can't call your parents?"

"*No.* The last time she came home drunk, they threatened to call the cops on her, and I believe them. They'll send her to jail."

"I just think—"

"Wait, do you see that?" Clara asked, inching ahead of me as she pointed off at the forest. It took me half a minute for my eyes to adjust, before finally making out an enormous, dark shape near the line of trees.

"I'm not angry with her," I whispered, my voice breaking. "I just want her to be okay. I just want—"

"Sh." Clara cut me off, leaning forward on her toes as she listened intently. She and I both heard the trickle of laughter coming from nearby at the same time, and we took off running. I quickly sped ahead of Clara, so I slowed down to grab her hand, keeping her up with me as we sprinted across the wet grass, hearing cracks of thunder ripple across the sky above us.

The white pickup truck came into view, but it barely registered in my brain. All I was focused on was the laughter filtering out of a ditch, too preoccupied to notice the open doors, or the shattered windshield, or the way Clara's hand slipped out of mine like a feather being lost to the wind.

I finally came to the pit, fumbling in my pocket for my cell phone before switching on the flashlight, taking in the ruffles of purple hair lying on the dirt, her head thrown back in laughter as a boy with brown hair lay still in front of her.

"She's drunk," I said stupidly. "She's been drinking, and she crashed her car."

"She's not drunk," Clara said from behind me, and I whirled around to shine my light on her, where she stood a good ten feet back, her face eerily neutral.

"What?" I demanded, my shoulders sagging with exhaustion. "What do you mean?"

"Taylor's not drunk, Aaron," Clara said again, squaring her shoulders. "She's on cocaine."

<u>**truth**</u>

How do you move forward?

After dragging your girlfriend and your teammate out of a ditch, buckling them into the backseats of your car, and letting them both (and Clara) stay the rest of the night at your house...

How do you recover from that?

I knew my relationship with Taylor wasn't over. She was far too incredible of a person to let go without an explanation, without a morning after, without the benefit of the doubt. But it felt like our light had been dimmed – like a thin cloud of disappointment had settled over me and coated the inside of my eyelids as I woke up the next morning.

The big game was Friday, and we were all supposed to be in school, but when I woke at noon, Clara was lying on my couch with Taylor and Devon curled up on the floor next to her, the coffee table pushed out into the hallway. I stepped over it as I peered into the living room, my lips tightening into a line as I took in the sight.

I checked my phone.

Mom, 7:14 AM: Hey honey, another shift

I closed my phone without reading the rest.

I didn't know what else to do, so I padded into the kitchen and switched on the stove, reaching into the refrigerator for a pat of butter. I began to cook, the salty smell of scrambled eggs wafting out into the living room, where I heard someone stir.

"Aaron," Clara's voice said from the doorway, and I glanced over at her briefly. She was still wearing the same black leggings and gray hoodie from the night before, but her chestnut-brown hair was tied up into a messy bun, exposing her grave face and intense eyes.

"Oh, your hair's up," I noted, returning my focus to the frypan. "I've never seen it like that before."

Clara was quiet.

"It looks nice," I elaborated. "Can you grab some forks?"

Twenty minutes later, four people were seated in a circle on my floor in front of the darkened TV, eating from steaming plates of eggs, bacon, and hashbrowns. Taylor's eyes remained fixed on the floor, looking like she was about to cry, whereas Devon's face remained blank, mindlessly staring at a wall. Clara, as per usual, kept her head low and her expression unreadable, which left me to initiate the conversation.

"Devon, I think you should leave," I said, and the brunette boy's head drifted over in my direction. "I won't tell the coaches about this, but I would just... really like you to go."

"Thanks for the food," Devon mumbled, grabbing his coat and pushing himself to his feet. He left quietly, slamming the door behind him, leaving the three of us in tension-filled silence once again.

"How often do you get high, Taylor?" I asked casually, spooning some eggs into my mouth. Taylor's shoulders stiffened, and she pushed her half-eaten plate away, curling her legs up into her chest.

"She's hungover, Aaron," Clara whispered quietly. "I'm not sure if now is the best time."

"I'm at least owed the courtesy of an explanation, or even an excuse," I said calmly, setting my plate down on the floor in front of me. "If she's hungover, all the better. That means you'll be more honest, right, Taylor?"

Taylor was silent for a good half minute before her muffled reply finally came: "my head hurts."

"Can you leave us alone?" Clara asked, nudging her elbow into my side. "Just for a minute."

I paused, thinking. "Just a minute," I conceded, standing and heading out into the hall.

Though I knew it was wrong, I lingered, waiting to overhear their conversation.

Taylor was speaking so quietly, it took me a while to be able to understand what she was saying, so I only caught the second half of their conversation:

"I'm already going to have to make up for this," Taylor murmured, still curled in on herself. "Now... don't you see, Clara? Aaron's different. He doesn't–"

"You chose him because he's different," Clara interrupted. "You pretended to be something you're not, and now your true colors are showing through. You can't blame anyone but yourself for that."

"I don't. It's just *hard*. So hard. And, God, my head–"

"I'm proud of you for trying, but this isn't right, Taylor. You're leading him on when you know any day now you could disappear, or worse–"

"I could go to rehab."

"Okay. Do that."

A pause. "I can't."

"I know."

Another long stretch of silence passed before Clara called out for me, and I sat back down beside her, staring at the top of Taylor's purple head as she hunched over, looking small and fragile. It hurt me, but all I could see was the blonde roots of her hair poking out and staring at me, reminding me that she was someone else beneath whatever exterior she had put up to fool other people.

"You do cocaine," I stated, my voice breaking. I cleared my throat, then continued. "You didn't tell me that you do drugs."

"You told me to bring things up naturally."

"Yeah, well, I guess there is no natural way to say you're an addict, right?"

Taylor's head snapped up, her dirty hair covering half of her face. "I'm not a–" she trailed off, and I sat back, drumming my fingers on my knees.

"Yeah, that's what I thought."

Clara was quiet, so I looked at her, and found her staring into the dark fireplace, her back to me.

"It started out with weed," Taylor murmured, and I turned to see her lying back down again, clutching at her hair. "Then it was ecstasy, then cocaine, then heroin."

My heart leapt in my chest.

"Now, it's all of them. All day. All the time. Never a moment sober, unless—"

I waited for her to go on, but she didn't.

"Unless she was with me," Clara finished for her, her head beginning to hang lower and lower. "She was sober with me, and then, she started being sober with you."

"It was so hard," Taylor wept, her voice shaking. "And the more time we spent together, it just got harder and harder. It felt impossible, so I started going hardcore whenever you weren't around. Late nights, early mornings, whatever. And with a junkie like Devon, too scared to try his first times alone—" she laughed humorlessly, "—it was like being given free access. Like someone above *wanted* me to reach this point."

"The dangerous point," I elaborated, still managing to keep my face neutral.

Taylor looked up again. "You make me want to be better, Aaron," she whispered, her nails digging into the soft skin of her thighs. "Being sober with you... didn't feel like I was being sober. I met you, and I wanted to start over, pretend I was – *could be* – this great person, and you were there, all perfect, and you *inspired* me. I wanted to go to college, to be successful… I wanted you. I still want you. I... I love you." Silent tears began to drip down her cheeks, and my heart ached. "But I can't change who I am. I can't give this up."

There was so much I wanted to say, but I just kept sitting there, watching her run her fingers over the grass stains on the Beatles shirt I'd given her, wet tears dripping down her cheeks.

"If I'm not worth enough for you to give up this toxic habit," I finally said, choosing my works carefully, "then this isn't going to work. At the end of the day, everyone will just be hurt." I scowled. "You crashed your car, Taylor. You crashed your car, and you were *laughing*. Drugs are destructive, and you'll just want to do more and more, and then what? You die? I'm not going to be around for that."

I swallowed, feeling like my chest was shattering into a million pieces. "I care about you so much, Taylor," I told her truthfully. "I want to help you, and I'm willing to stick around, if you agree to get better. To *try*. You don't just have to be that perfect girl temporarily. You can be her all the time, and I know you want that. It takes work, though. It takes work, and it's going to be hard, but I'm here for you every step of the way."

A pause.

"And if I don't want to change?" Taylor squeaked, hiding her face. "To get better?"

"Then I'm out," I sighed resignedly, knowing I was making the right decision. "I can't force you to be anything, or anyone, you don't want to be, but I'm tired of nights like these. Not knowing where you are, all this lying – I won't deal with that Taylor any longer. Not a single second more." I felt tears bubbling up in my eyes, and quickly blinked them away. "Bring back the Taylor from the ice cream shop. The Taylor who drove eight miles just for barbecue – the Taylor who likes her coffee black, and her water without lemon... the Taylor who promised me that I'd never see that other Taylor again."

I sucked in a deep breath before continuing. "The Taylor," I murmured, reaching out to take her hand, "that's the toughest, smartest, most beautiful girl I know. Not the Taylor I found in the ditch last night."

"Speaking of which," Clara mumbled, pushing herself to her feet and stepping towards the hallway. "I'll call someone to tow the truck." I watched her go, then returned my focus to stroking the back of Taylor's knuckle with my thumb, leaning to try and catch her eye.

"What do you say?" I asked, praying for her to make the right decision. "Which Taylor will you choose?"

The minutes Taylor spent thinking were the most agonizing of my life. I listened to Clara talking quietly on the phone in the kitchen, the birds singing outside, and the rustling of the trees. I listened, and I waited. I busied myself by preparing for either answer, no matter how hard it was to accept the fact that Taylor might not want to get better.

Finally, she spoke.

"I'm going to do it." Taylor raised her head and looked at me, her brown eyes meeting mine.

"Do what?" I whispered, feeling like I had no air in my lungs.

"I'm going to try."

practice

The big game was in 24 hours, and Taylor had been sober for three days.

Therefore, I had not been in school all week.

"How are you doing?" I asked, leaning over Taylor as I propped up her pillow. We didn't dare ask her parents for help, and Clara had tried to take over the duties herself, but it turned out that Taylor was a bigger job now. She broke out in cold sweats, scratched at her arms until they bled, and once tried to make a break for a hidden stash.

Luckily, she was doing better; eating more, and sleeping longer, which is why I decided it would be all right to go to the last football practice before the game.

"I'm leaving," I told Clara, reaching in my pocket for my car keys. "Text me if anything's up, okay?"

"I will," Clara assured me, hurrying behind me into Taylor's bedroom. I left with a feeling of dread in my stomach, not so much for Taylor, but for my coaches, who I'd have to explain my *many* absences to.

I pulled into the parking lot of the stadium, smiling to myself as my eyes landed on the clusters of players warming up on the field. I grabbed my bag from the backseat of the MINI and headed for the entrance, hoping I'd be able to slip by without my coaches noticing.

They noticed.

"Parker!" Coach Brett barked, waving me over to where he and Coach Caputo were standing on the sidelines. Like a scared puppy, I hung my head and jogged over to where they were standing, brainstorming up a detailed excuse in my head.

To my surprise, they didn't yell at me, or threaten my position as quarterback, or even bring up my absence at all. Instead, Coach Caputo said, "There's someone we want you to meet."

I opened my mouth to speak, then closed it, nodding as I followed the coaches over to the water coolers.

"This is Joe Lindbergh," Coach Brett told me, gesturing to the player behind him. He was African American, and stood a good few inches taller than me, his shoulders impossibly broad. The second we locked eyes, I could tell he wasn't just any football player. "He just transferred over from Darcy High. I thought you two should get to know each other."

"Coach?" I questioned, breaking my stare to look at the two middle-aged men in confusion.

"He's our new star. He can play any position, including receiver, so, as our quarterback, I figured you two should spend the day together. Show him how we do things here."

"Nice to meet you," I said politely, holding my hand out for Joe to shake. He took it, crushing it in a bone-shattering grip, before leaning in to slap me on the back.

"Good to be working with you, *partner*," he said, his voice deep and husky. "So, you're the famous Aaron Parker I've heard so much about?"

I glanced over my shoulder to see the coaches backing away, giving us our space.

"I don't know what you've heard," I said coolly, pulling on my gear.

"That you're a punk ass that can't even be bothered to show up for practice."

My head snapped up, my lips turning down into a scowl. "Excuse me?"

"Yeah, I know. You think you can just skate by because you're naturally talented, but that isn't the case anymore. It's scouting season, and if you want any kind of shot at a scholarship, you'll give this team the time and energy it deserves."

I was shocked into silence.

"Let's get to work, then," Joe said, tossing me a football, "*partner.*"

***

The next three hours became a one-on-one match between me and Joe. We kept trying to outdo each other, sprinting farther and faster and throwing harder and longer, so, by the time the end of practice rolled around, my rusty muscles were practically screaming from the abuse.

"Good practice," Joe complimented me as we finished up at the water coolers. "You've certainly got skills."

"And I'm willing to work hard," I assured him, staring at him over the lid of my water bottle as sweat dripped down the ends of my hair. "I'm not going to make excuses."

"That's what it takes."

I smirked. "What are you, some kind of football guru?"

"I'm nineteen years old," he said, and my stomach dropped, along with my smile. "I may be a dumbass, but I've been around the block, so I know some things about this kind of life." He looked out over the field, his eyes soft. "Now that I'm at this school, I'm going to have to keep my grades up to stay on the team, so I'll finally graduate, and you'll be alone next year, partner." He slapped my shoulder with his enormous, gloved hand. "You need to leave the personal shit out. The world's getting more and more competitive. If you want to come out on top, football has to be your number one priority."

I was silent, thinking about Taylor.

"Nice job today," Joe said, then turned around, and left.

***

When I got back to the Lawson house, I felt refreshed. Rejuvenated, even. Football normally left me in a happy mood, but, after my interactions with Joe, I felt even more inspired than normal. I took his transfer as a sign that things were getting better – Taylor was safe, sober, and I could finally return my focus to my greatest passion.

"Hey, so, I was thinking," I told Taylor, brushing her sweaty hair out of her face. "What if you tried sports? Something to keep you preoccupied."

Taylor was quiet. "I used to play softball," she whispered.

"Sounds perfect," I told her. "As soon as you're feeling better, I'll go with you to the field at school. Sound good?"

"Definitely," she murmured, sounding weak.

"You think you can come to my game tomorrow?"

"Of course," she said, sounding stronger. She even pushed her head up to look at me, smiling reassuringly. "I wouldn't miss it for the world."

I grinned. "Good," I said.

game

The big day.

The stands were packed even hours before the coin toss. It was the Homecoming game, so proposals were being made left and right, and I found myself particularly impressed by a guy that got a whole row of people to hold up signs that spelled out 'Sasha?'

Maybe I should ask Taylor, I thought to myself. She wasn't really one for school dances, but she did like romantic gestures, so I began to brainstorm ideas with Levi and some other teammates.

"Like, when you're getting interviewed, ask her into the mic," Steve, a porky lineman, suggested as I doused myself with cold water.

"Need a fallback plan, since they'll most likely be interviewing Joe," I told them, nodding at the giant standing a few yards away. "He's gonna steal the show tonight."

"Man, don't be so modest!" Levi cried, plopping down on the ground to stretch his legs. "The media will be *all over* you. We're projected to be #1 in the state! That's big, dude."

"I'm just glad you made it onto the team," I joked. "Without you here, I'd be stuck with Coach Caput-no and his *inspiring* speeches of wisdom."

"Listen up, everyone!" Coach Brett shouted from behind us, and I turned to see him dangerously standing on a foldout table. "Coach Caputo has a few words he'd like to say before the coin toss!"

I rolled my eyes. "*Great.*"

"That was crazy, dude!" Levi chirped excitedly as we began to circle up. Levi was always excited. "You said it, and then it happened! You're magic, bro. It's a good sign."

"I hope so," I murmured, putting my head in the huddle. "I can certainly use some luck right now."

***

Looking for Taylor in the crowd was one of the many times I was glad she had bright purple hair.

Where?? I texted Clara. *I swear 2 god, I can't see u anywhere.*

how many goddamn concession stands are there, we're right above it

There r like 3 concession stands, not including the merch store

what kind of school is this

I smiled down at my phone before looking up to search the crowded bleachers again. The coin toss was about to go down, so I knew I'd have to head onto the field soon. Suddenly, my phone was ringing in my hand.

"Hello?" I asked, still scanning around for Taylor and Clara.

"Okay, so, the sign next to us says 'Upperclassmen'," Clara said, her voice crackly over the phone. "See us?"

I found the sign, then laughed. "Is there a huge dude sitting in front of you guys?"

"You found us!"

"I did, I just can't *see* you."

"Well, we can see you, and that's what's important." I heard Taylor in the background. "I'm going to give you to your girlfriend now." I waited patiently, and couldn't help but smile at the sound of Taylor's voice.

"Hey, babe," she cooed, her voice audibly shaking.

"You okay?" I asked, glaring at Levi as he made kissy faces with Steve.

"Fine. I'm cold as hell, though." I heard her laugh. "Whose idea was it to have the season this late in the year?"

"There's always spring football."

"You are *not* dragging me out here for the next five months, Aaron Parker."

"We'll see about that, Taylor Lawson." I covered the mic to address my teammates. "If you guys don't fuck off right exactly now, I'll shove my foot so far up your—"

"Just wanted to tell you good luck," Taylor said, sounding tired. "My Snapchat story's going to be, like, an hour long. We can watch it later."

"Sounds good. And the cookout?"

"I'm *so* there. Clara is, too. You think we'd miss a late night meat fest?"

The referee blew his whistle, and I scrambled for my helmet. "I gotta go. That's my signal."

"You're on the big screen! Look up!"

"I *can't*." I laughed. "See you later. Love you."

"Break a leg! Love you, too."

As I shoved past Levi towards the field, a roar of applause rose up from the stands behind me. I took the time to glance up at the Jumbotron, where, sure enough, my helmeted face was shining with sweat as I jogged out to the fifty-yard line.

I sidled up next to Coach Brett, then took a moment to breathe in the atmosphere before the game. That exact moment was why I played — I fed off the anticipation in the air. The crowd's excitement, the screaming in my ears as I savored each and every second out on that field.

"Call it," the referee said to me.

"Heads," I said. It'd always been my lucky side.

"Gunnison captain Aaron Parker calls 'heads'," the referee reported into his mic, stepping up to initiate the toss.

Holding my breath, I watched as he flipped.

***

Throughout the game, I kept checking Taylor and Clara's spot, and was pleased when the enormous man in front of them moved seats so

I could get an eyeful. Taylor looked exhausted, the bags under her eyes visible even from where I was standing. But, with her hair tied back into a ponytail and one of my t-shirts hugged around her thin form, she was the most beautiful person in the stands.

Clara was sitting beside her, closely monitoring everything she did. I noticed the way she glanced over at Taylor after every play, as if she expected her to bolt at any moment. My heart lurched to jump over the railings and join them, but I had a duty to fulfill, and a future to secure.

Joe and I made quite the team. By the time halftime rolled around, we were up 14-0 against the Frawley High Foxes, and I sat down beside him in the locker room as the band marched out onto the field.

"Did you know they made me co-captain?" Joe asked, squirting his water bottle into his mouth. I raised an eyebrow.

"No, I didn't," I said.

"I thought you should hear before it gets out. It just happened." He glanced over at me, his coal-black eyes shining with the glow of the stadium lights.

"Pretty impressive for a transfer."

"Hard work, Aaron. It'll get you far." He smiled. "Here's to the second half."

"The second half," I agreed, pulling out my phone.

From Taylor, 9:04 PM: Ur butt looks good in those pants.

I grinned.

Admit it, I texted. *Ur having fun.*

Am not. I'm miserable. Clara won't get me popcorn.

Tell her my wallet's in my car. She has the keys.

Ur the best.

I know.

I headed back out onto the field just in time to see Taylor stand from the bleachers and hurry down the steps, waving at me as she rounded the corner to the staircase leading down to the area beneath the stands. My eyes returned to Clara, who was watching her go with a furrowed brow.

From Clara, 9:07 PM: she took your keys from me

I told her she could get my wallet 4 food, but it's good to know youd be virtually useless if she ever were 2 actually bolt.

idk if that was a good idea

What, popcorn? Ur the one always telling me not 2 stress. Just relax & have some fun.

The whistle blew.

I have to go. Lmk when Taylor gets back.

will do

Before I hurried out, I sent Taylor a quick text:

U sneak. I meant for Clara to go get it, not u. Get back soon, 2nd half starting.

My brow furrowed as a notice popped up, but I had no time to dwell over it before I had to get to my teammates. I left my phone on the bench, the message following me all the way out on the field.

Not delivered.

<u>**end**</u>

After the third quarter, Taylor still wasn't back.

I blinked as my eyes landed on the empty seat next to Clara, who was looking equally as unnerved as I was. She kept pulling out her phone to check it, and I did the same with mine.

When Clara caught me looking, she waved wildly and smiled brightly, breaching out of her shell of shyness for a moment. I had a feeling that the stadium was her happy place, too.

At the beginning of the fourth quarter, I texted Clara.

Is she back yet?

The answer came immediately.

no.

Sighing, I tossed my phone at my bag and ran my hands through my hair. The stress had caused me to perform poorly, so I was benched for a few plays while the 2nd string quarterback took over. We were now neck and neck with Frawley, with the score being 21-21.

"Your hands are shaking," Joe noted, dropping his helmet at my feet. I exhaled loudly before forcing out my best, most confident smile.

"I'm fine," I assured him.

"It isn't the game," Joe said, more of a statement than a question. "Remember, leave the personal shit at home."

"The problem is, I brought it here," I burst, the words exploding out of my mouth before I could stop them.

Joe's mouth tightened. "You mean, you brought her here."

I nodded bleakly, feeling ashamed.

"The only thing you can do is focus on the positives," Joe advised, pulling his helmet back on. "Get a better outlook."

As he jogged away, I decided he was right, and began to make a chart in my head.

Things NOT to think about:

•*where Taylor is*

•*the possibility of losing to Frawley*

•*where Taylor is*

•*Joe being co-captain*

•*where Taylor is*

Things to focus on:

•*Clara's here*

•*I'm about to kick some ass.*

As the coach beckoned me out to the field, I pulled on my helmet and steeled my nerves.

Time to win this thing.

***

There were only twenty seconds left, and Frawley was winning 24-21.

Sweat was pouring down my face, and every inch of me ached. My arms, my back, my legs – *especially* my head. I'd thrown myself into the game, and had gotten us all the way down to the 4-yard line, but I was running out of time.

My gaze landed on Joe, who was ready and waiting to pounce. We locked eyes, and he nodded, communicating with me silently. I sucked in a deep breath before letting it out slowly, waiting for the play to begin.

The roar of the crowd faded into the background, replaced by a dull hiss that took root in my ears and swallowed my entire being completely. In a single second, I calculated every single move I could make, and knew there was only one thing to do.

I grabbed the ball, and I ran.

Normally, it was me throwing the ball to receivers for touchdowns, and I'd never actually scored one myself. But, with bodies falling on me left and right, I powered through, digging my heels into the soft grass as I propelled myself over the line.

As the clock ran out, I scored the final touchdown of the game, leading Gunnison High to a victory of 27-24.

I let myself go limp as my teammates tackled me to the ground, screaming and whooping victoriously. My entire being hurt, and I just wanted to go home and curl up with Taylor.

Taylor. Everything I had blocked out came rushing in all at once, and I felt myself panicking. I leapt out of the congratulatory pile and shoved my way through the crowd, my eyes raising to where students were climbing over the railings to storm the field.

And there, right next to the 'Upperclassmen' sign, sat Clara, the seat beside her still empty.

As I was swept away in a flow of adoring fans and teachers, I began to sob. Tears exploded out of my eyes as I knelt to the ground, pressing my hands to my eyes in a futile attempt to stop the flow.

Aw, how cute, the voices around me chorused. *He's so happy, he's crying.*

If only they knew the truth.

***

I stayed for a few interviews after I'd collected myself, remaining professional and courteous, and making sure to highlight Joe's amazing performance as well as my team's. Everyone began to go home, including my parents, who I'd told to start the cookout without me.

Soon, the field was completely deserted. I emerged out of the locker room, freshly showered with my football bag, and looked up to see Clara still rooted to the same spot in the bleachers, stiff as a board.

My heart in my throat, I climbed over the railing and started up into the stands, my footsteps echoing impossibly loudly around the empty stadium.

As I approached, I realized that Clara was staring out across the field, her blue eyes filled with something unidentifiable. I sat down next to her and set my bag at our feet, joining her in her silence.

"She's never coming back," Clara croaked, her voice as broken as we both felt.

"I know," I whispered, silent tears streaming down my cheeks as I pulled her to my chest. "I know."

There, in that empty stadium, as the lights powered down on what was supposed to be the greatest day of my life, we cried.

rebuilding

I quit my job at the ice cream shop.

Everywhere I went was *her*. *Her* car. *Her* coffee. I wasn't sure I'd ever be able to look directly at the color purple again.

I threw myself into football. Scheduling private practices, calling spontaneous meetings with Joe – I went at it 24/7. After that first night, I didn't allow myself to cry. I shoved everything down and prayed for it all to dissolve away, the pain lying just beneath the surface of my hard exterior. I smiled less, and found I'd lost my sense of humor. Some people noticed, but decided not to comment on it. After all, Taylor's disappearance had spread all over the school, and everyone knew.

I had just settled into my new routine when, one afternoon, right as practice was ending, I looked up into the stands and saw Clara.

After showering, I headed up to join her beneath the gray skies, realizing she was sitting in the same row she'd been in during the night of the homecoming game.

She was the first to speak. "I'm not doing so well," she admitted, staring off across the field.

I sat down next to her, unsure of what to say. "Neither am I," I told her, running my hands over the rough fabric of my jeans.

"I finished my book," Clara whispered, pulling her blue notebook out of her messenger bag. I watched as she leafed through the pages lovingly, her eyes roaming over the rows upon rows of spidery handwriting.

When she came to the end, to my surprise, she ripped out the last page and folded it in half, pressing it against the cold metal of the bleacher before sliding it over to me.

"Is it about Taylor?" I murmured, unsure if I was ready for that.

"No," Clara told me, standing up and shouldering her bag. "It's about you."

I stayed sitting as she headed down the bleachers and left, leaving me alone with the howling wind and monochromatic sky.

I unfolded the piece of paper, my jaw involuntarily clenching as I began to read.

He is strong.

There are many things special about him. He is talented, and hardworking, and handsome, but the one thing that makes him beautiful is his strength.

He is strong not because of the metal he lifts, or the sport he plays. He is strong because he carries a much larger weight every day. It is powerful, and heavy, and so invisible I'm not certain if even he knows it's there.

But I see him. I see the way he closes his locker door with slow fingers, the way his strides are long and uncertain as he walks down the hall. I see it all, because I carry a similar weight, and I want him to know that he is not alone.

Meet me for coffee tomorrow at 1.

With understanding,

Clara

And then I was crying again.

<u>**notebook**</u>

"You said, 'meet me for *coffee*', *not* hot chocolate."

"I don't like coffee. And anyway, I didn't technically write it to *you*, I wrote it to the mystery man in the last page of my book."

"Oh, shut up." I grinned, watching Clara blush under my gaze as her thin fingers circled around her Styrofoam cup of hot chocolate. "How are you doing?"

"Well, I'm going shopping for a new notebook today." She reached into her messenger bag and pulled out a yellow post-it. "These are the colors I'm thinking of."

I took the note, then barked with laughter. "You had to *write down* what colors you want? As if you'll forget?"

She scowled at me as I continued to chuckle. "Oh, hush up. This is something I'll have for the next few months; it's important."

"I'm sorry, I'm sorry. Okay. Yes. Let's see... definitely *not* orange."

"Why not?! It's bright, and fun."

"*Orange*, Clara."

"Fine. Next one."

"Red. Hmm. That could be doable."

"Since I went black, then yellow, then blue, I figured I should pick a lighter color."

"Yeah, that sounds like your style."

Her eyebrows flew up. "And what exactly *is* my style?"

"You know."

"No, I don't." She sat back, an amused smile playing on her lips.

"Ooh, I like this one, though," I murmured, tracing my fingers over her handwriting.

"Which?"

"Light blue. Like your eyes."

She wrinkled her nose at me. "Light blue it is, then."

I crumpled the note up and tossed it at her head, which she caught expertly.

"Taylor wasn't the only one who played softball," she explained, laughing at my shocked expression.

***

As we roamed the aisles of *Jetson's Office Supplies*, the conversation gradually turned from notebooks and hot chocolate to more serious topics. I don't remember the transition, but found myself somewhat relieved that we were beginning to dissect the elephant in the room.

"I don't miss her as much as I probably should," Clara murmured as she trailed her fingertips over the endless rows of spines, her back to me, "since she was never around, anyway. Does that make me a bad person?"

"Of course not," I assured her, inspecting a nearby notebook. "I haven't given myself enough time to miss her. I guess I do, though."

"No one could have helped her," Clara whispered, turning around to look into my face. "You know that, right?"

I swallowed, blinking back a sudden wave of tears. "Yeah," I said softly. "Yeah."

"I feel like... I feel like I triggered her relapse," Clara mumbled, and my eyebrows shot up.

"What?" I asked incredulously.

"That day in the coffee shop..." she rubbed her arm in discomfort, "after I screamed at our tutoring session, I told Taylor it was her fault. I regret it so much – I was so awful to her."

"Clara, *you* were the triggered one," I reminded her. "Taylor was already using, and it wasn't you. It wasn't you at all."

She smiled tightly, but I could tell she didn't believe me. I was about to say something else when her gaze fell onto the shelf behind me, where her eyes widened. "That one."

I turned and spied a light blue notebook hidden beneath a stack of black hardcover ones. "Really? The sticker says it's used."

"I know." Clara stood on her toes to grab the book before leafing through the pages, a smile appearing on her lips when she came upon what was left of ripped out pages. "All of my books have to have imperfections. Besides, it's only a dollar."

"Cheap, for a book of that size." I grinned at her as she hugged it to her chest. "What was wrong with the other three you had?"

"The blue one had this huge ink stain on the inside of the front cover, the yellow one had been scribbled on by some kid, and the black one I found on the street when I was thirteen."

I stared at her, impressed.

"I knew immediately," she said, holding her new notebook out in front of her to admire it.

"Pick one out for me, then," I told her, nodding at the shelves. "I think it's time I faced everything head-on, even if I'm not much of a writer."

Clara offered me a small smile. "If you really want to, then what about that one?" She pointed down the aisle, where I searched for what she was looking at. "I mean, you don't have to, of course. It's just–"

"No," I sighed, pulling the purple notebook out of its place. "It's fine. It's perfect, actually."

Clara held out her hand to lead me to the register.

"We'll get through this, Aaron," she told me. "Together."

No words had ever sounded better.

<u>library</u>

It was getting colder, so Clara told me she'd started writing in the local library, which was where I found her one day after school, her nose buried in her new notebook.

I slipped into the seat across from her, waiting for her to look up. It took seven minutes.

"Holy Jesus!" She cried, startling so violently she nearly fell out of her chair. "*Aaron?*"

"No, I'm his long-lost twin, Archie."

"I mean, I saw you sit down, but I don't ever look up, since it's awkward if it's someone I don't know, and... I just... you *fucker*!" She leaned across the table to punch me in the shoulder. I gasped dramatically.

"I'm *crushed*, Clara."

She grinned as she flipped the cover of her book shut. "Why didn't you tell me you were coming?"

"I wanted to surprise you."

"Well, you certainly did."

"What are you writing today?"

She narrowed her eyes at me. "I've only shown you my writing twice. What makes you think that would be a regular thing?"

"Because it's a special occasion."

"Oh, yeah?" She leaned forward, her blue eyes shining beneath the fluorescent lights. "And why's that?"

"Because they found my mom's car," I said meekly, my lips tightening as I waited for her reaction.

As my words sank in, Clara sat back, blinking rapidly.

"It was in Arizona," I told her, running my hands through my hair. "The plates were different, and it'd been left in a ditch somewhere off of a desert road."

"A-Are you sure it was yours?" Clara sputtered, her face as white as a sheet.

"Yep. I just need to brush off the dust, and I'll finally have it back."

"That's... great." Clara forced out a smile, evidently unnerved.

"Tell you what," I told her, resting my elbows on the table. "You share yours, and I'll share mine."

Her expression instantly transformed. "You've been writing?"

"A *lot*." I found a hot blush creeping up my neck. "It's crap, but I just can't seem to stop. I never realized how much I keep to myself."

"Yeah, it's surprising." She unsuccessfully attempted to force down her involuntary grin. "Did your hand start cramping?"

"Oh, like you wouldn't *believe*."

"Yeah, you'll be able to go longer and longer the more you do it." Her eyes lit up as she talked about her passion, finally able to relate with someone. "My cure is soaking my hand in hot water. Not cold, or your muscles will tighten up."

"Thanks for the tip," I told her. "I also have this problem where the ink smears."

"Use a less watery pen. I've started writing in pencil." She reached into her bag and pulled out an expensive-looking mechanical pencil, sparing it one last look before sliding it across the table to me. "A gift."

"I couldn't," I cried.

"You could, and you will." We grinned. "Just take it. I have, like, a dozen others."

I accepted it warily, watching as she reached into her bag for her book.

"I have something, but it's not very good," she murmured modestly. "You first."

"Okay," I told her, pulling my purple notebook out of my backpack. "Mine is a trillion times worse, though."

I watched her eyes roam over the stammering verses of poetry I'd managed to slap down onto the page, her smile growing wider and wider.

"It's great," she assured me. "I think you meant 'belligerent' with an i, not b-e-l-l-e."

"Thanks," I said. "Now, fork yours over."

"Fuck," she whispered, her smile betraying her hesitant tone. "Do I have to?"

"Yes. Hand it here."

She sighed as she passed the light blue notebook across the table, watching nervously as I turned to the bookmarked page.

She wore her headphones for so long they began to hurt her ears.

Music was her passion — the world, her instrument. Drumming on the subway seats, whistling at the birds perched atop streetlamps, composing grand symphonies in her head even when silence was forced upon her. The commotion of the city couldn't drown out her music, but he could.

Every time he hit her, she imagined the ivory on a piano breaking, cracking more and more until she was certain she wouldn't be able to stand it for another second. She grabbed her guitar and took to the streets, sleeping in cardboard boxes during the night and playing for the masses throughout the day. Caked in dust and grime, she was the happiest she'd ever been.

She vowed to never let anyone take her music away again.

"Wow," I breathed, longing for more. "Do you only write these short pieces?"

"Sometimes," Clara admitted, reaching to take the notebook back from me. "Half of my last book was the makings of a novel, but I don't have that kind of patience."

I grinned. "I could read your writing forever."

"Let's stick with special occasions," Clara chirped, slipping out of her chair. "Now, come on. I want to see the car."

car wash

"I thought seeing it might give me some sort of closure," Clara murmured, staring at the car with an unreadable expression on her face. "I thought... I don't know what I thought."

My eyes flickered from her face to the MINI, its entire exterior thickly veiled with layers upon layers of red dust. I swallowed as memories hit me in the face like a slap – driving Taylor home, on dates, her purple hair fluttering with the breeze of the air conditioning...

"Let's take it for a wash," I suggested, snapping myself back to reality. Clara eyed me incredulously. "I mean it." The more I talked, the more appealing the idea sounded. "What's more fun than driving through a car wash?"

"Scrub everything away," Clara went on, evidently coming around.

"Yeah! Let's go!" I hopped in the driver's seat and turned my new key in the ignition, waiting for Clara to climb into the passenger seat.

We drove to a place a few minutes away called 'Sam's Pitstop', which consisted of a rundown gas station with a fully-automated car wash extending off the side of the main building. I paused at the payment station, paid, then pulled up to the opening, where I found a neon arrow pointing to the track system.

"You ready?" I asked Clara, grinning mischievously as I prepared to shift forward.

"Definitely," Clara responded, smiling softly.

I put the gear in neutral and braced myself against the seat as the car jerked forward, waiting for the cycle to begin. Enormous geysers of white began washing over the exterior of the MINI, whisking away the red dust and caking the car in goo.

"Wow," Clara breathed. I looked over to see her gazing out the window in wonder, sitting forward in her seat.

"This is only the pre-soak," I said, smirking at her excitement, and kept my eyes on her as we continued on through the next stage. I watched as her lips parted in surprise throughout the scrubbing and cleaning, her fingers gripping the armrest of the seat. The Clara in front of me was completely different from the Clara around other people, the shy Clara that hid behind her hair and skipped class out of anxiety. Now, this Clara had her brilliant eyes fixed on the windows, her hair tucked behind her ears as she let herself go. She was beginning to trust me, and, in a world of unpredictability and hardship, it was nice to have an ally.

As the water ran over the glass in blurry, amorphous streams, Clara relaxed into her seat, hugging her arms around her. Her gaze lowered again.

"Taylor moved too fast for this sort of thing," Clara murmured, reaching up to stroke the ends of her hair. "She'd be bored right now, asking when we could go get Burger King."

"I know," I said, smiling at the thought. "The thing is, Taylor didn't take *any* time to slow down. She didn't appreciate the little things, like getting your car washed. She tried, I'll give her that, but it's just not who she was." I looked out the window. "*Is*. And wherever she is... I just hope she's happy."

Right then, in that car wash, I finally began to feel better.

***

"Thanks for today, Aaron," Clara told me, shutting the door and leaning in through the passenger window. "I really needed it."

"No problem," I said, drumming my fingers on the wheel. "Let's do it again sometime."

"Definitely." She grinned and began to back away from the car, waiting for me to switch gears before turning and hurrying up to her house.

As I drove home, I began to think about the practice I'd scheduled with Levi tomorrow, and pulled out my phone when I came to a red light.

Hey man, just wondering if we could reschedule. I could rly use a break.

He responded almost immediately. *Sure dude! U earned it. Text u later*

I smiled softly as I looked down at my phone, slipping it back into my pocket when the light changed. It was only when I looked up that I realized I was by the ice cream shop, the neon 'open' sign blaring right next to my window. Swallowing, I stared at the dimly-lit store, my thoughts racing, unaware that I'd completely frozen at a green light.

A honk sounded from behind me, and I startled, racing to lurch forward around the corner. Before I knew what was happening, I'd veered into the empty parking lot and shut off the MINI, breathing heavily as I climbed out of the car.

I started towards the shop with my hands in my pockets, my breath filtering out in front of me in tiny wisps of fog. I caught sight of black hair behind the counter, and faltered near the entrance, remembering how I'd quit over text.

"Sara," I called, my voice muffled through the glass. She turned around expectantly, her expression falling at the sight of me.

"Well, come in," she beckoned, waving me on. I lowered my eyes and placed my hand on the knob, steeling my nerves.

I pulled the door open and stepped inside, breathing in the familiar sugary scent.

"What can I get for you?" Sara asked, turning her back to me. "Since you're obviously not here to work."

"I wanted to apologize, Sara," I told her earnestly. "I've been having a rough time... I'm sorry."

She paused, evidently waiting for me to go on.

"I'm not ready to come back to work," I continued, my voice breaking, "but I'm here."

"That's a step," Sara said over her shoulder.

"Something's blocking me," I murmured, running my hands through my hair. "Sorry, I don't know why I'm telling you this, it's just... I feel stuck. You know?"

She turned around. "Aaron," she murmured. "What can I get for you?"

My heart leapt into my throat. "Vanilla with purple sprinkles," I whispered. "To stay."

<u>attack</u>

I'd planned to have lunch with Clara at a new diner that had opened up on the other side of town, but I was running ten minutes late.

I parked my car in the lot and headed towards the front, hoping Clara had scored a table for us. The place looked packed.

As soon as I pushed in the door, I could sense something was wrong. The atmosphere was heavy, eerily quiet for such an enormous crowd. Bodies were jammed into seats at the bar, in booths, at tables – there were at least seventy people, maybe more.

And it was dead silent.

Realizing everyone's heads were turned in the direction of the TVs, my brow knitted together in a line, my gaze landing on Clara. She was standing on her tiptoes near the bar, her hands clutched to her chest. Her face was sheet-white.

"Clara," I muttered, trying not to disturb the tense aura. "*Clara.*"

I tugged on her sleeve, forgetting myself, but, surprisingly, she didn't even seem to notice.

I stepped forward to join her at her side, my gaze dropping down to her face. She was staring at the TV with a shocked expression, her icy blue eyes wider than I'd ever seen them before.

"Wh–" My gaze finally found the television, where a frazzled-looking news reporter was speaking into a handheld mic.

"...death count has now risen to 100," she was saying, her blonde hair billowing around in the wind. "Reporting to you live – 100 dead, hundreds injured in Paris attacks, where suicide bombers struck the *Stade de France*, and gunmen opened fire at neighboring cafés in central Paris."

"Oh... oh my God," I sputtered, staring at the headlines in disbelief.

"We'll keep you updated – we have a cell phone video posted to Twitter showing fans storming the stadium field as explosions–"

"Oh, Clara, don't look," I whispered, wrapping my hand around the small girl's eyes. "Let's get you out of here..."

I pushed through the throng of people towards the entrance, leading Clara blindly. She leaned against me heavily, her arms limp at her sides.

As we burst out into the frigid November air, Clara began mumbling something under her breath, and I sat her down on the curb.

"*The guns... guns... the guns...*" Clara whispered, her eyes fixed on the ground. I cupped her face in my hands to try and get her to look at me, but her breathing was becoming more and more rapid, a panic attack evidently about to overtake her.

"Hey, Clara," I cooed soothingly, but it was clear she couldn't hear me. There was a wild, animalistic fear in her eyes, something so raw and foreign that I immediately pulled away.

"*Guns... guns...* eyes!" With the last word, Clara began rocking back and forth, pressing her palms to her face. "Oh, God... oh, God..."

"Clara, I'm right here with y–"

She shrieked loudly, cutting me off.

"No!" Suddenly, she shot to her feet and attempted to sprint off down the sidewalk. I quickly grabbed onto her and pulled her to my chest, gripping her tightly as she struggled in my arms.

"Clara!" I yelped, panic rising up into my throat. There was no Taylor to come to the rescue. No understanding friend I could call. There was no *time*, and it was just me, my hold on Clara loosening more and more as she thrashed.

The small girl tore at her face with her fingers, screaming unintelligibly. It took all my strength to drag her into a nearby alley, pinning her up against the grimy brick wall.

"Please, don't," she sobbed, grabbing onto my hand. "*Please...*"

"Clara, it's me," I whispered, keeping my hands on her shoulders as she slid down to the ground. "It's Aaron."

"They're dead," she whispered, curling in on herself. I grabbed her hand and began stroking it, desperately willing her to calm down. I had zero experience in that type of situation, and didn't have a clue of how to react, or what to do.

Suddenly, Clara went silent, streams of tears dripping down her pained face. Her mouth was open in a silent yell of agony, her entire body trembling violently.

For a moment, she was back to her old self, fighting through her tears and pain to lock eyes with me. "Why do people do that, Aaron?" She croaked, digging her fingernails into her legs. "Why do people kill?"

"I don't know," I whispered truthfully, gathering her into my arms. "I really don't know."

145

I pressed her head to my chest and closed my eyes as she grabbed onto my shirt, *feeling* her, rather than listening. I felt the way her chest heaved up and down; the way her thin, bony legs curled around my own. I felt the pain rolling off of her in waves, and wanted nothing more than to ease her burden, even if only for a moment.

"What can I do?" I begged, struggling to keep my voice even. "How can I help?"

"I want to go home," Clara wept, burying her face in my neck. "Please, take me home."

Without waiting for her to say anything else, I scooped her up into my arms and carried her down the sidewalk, listening to her cry all the way.

***

"Soup," I murmured, handing the mug in my hands to Clara. "It's not as good as yours, of course, but it's all I had."

Clara was sitting on the couch in her living room, staring off into the distance as I wrapped her in layers upon layers of fluffy blankets. She'd stopped sobbing, but her cries were replaced by an eerie, stony silence, and I wasn't sure which I preferred.

"If you're not hungry, I can make you something else," I offered, watching her set the cup down on the coffee table. "I don't know what you have in the pantry, but I can go check—"

"Aaron," Clara rasped, her voice hoarse and broken. "Sit down."

I sat, looking on as she tucked her hair behind her ears and ran her fingertips over the scratches on her face. She paused, retreating back into herself, and I blinked quietly, wondering how to proceed.

146

I'd just glanced over at the TV when she spoke again.

"Did you know I hate vanilla ice cream?"

My mouth opened, then shut.

"I hate it," she murmured, picking at a loose thread on one of the blankets. "It's just so flavorless, and it tastes like sugary paper more than anything."

I didn't dare speak.

"When Taylor and I visited you at the ice cream shop, she always ordered for me." Her jaw clenched. "She thought she was doing me a favor, because of my anxiety, but she never once bothered to ask me what flavor I wanted." She smiled grimly, a single tear dripping down her cheek. "I think about that a lot."

I slowly moved over, touching my knee with hers.

"I like birthday cake." She was crying harder now. "Birthday cake ice cream is my favorite."

I slowly draped my arms around her shoulders and pulled her to me, stroking her hair gently as her tears soaked through my shirt.

We stayed like that for a long time.

unblock

"Hey, Sara," I said to the dark-haired woman, leaning on the counter as I watched her towel off a scooper. "The usual, please."

"I haven't hired a permanent replacement, you know." She pushed the ice cream across the counter, arching an eyebrow. "But I won't keep using temps forever. Even if you were a shit employee… it's been over a month, Aaron."

"I know," I sighed, sliding a five-dollar bill across the counter. "I just need a little more time. That's all I'm asking."

"I like you, Aaron," Sara sighed, "and I feel bad about what happened, but I'm going to start handing out applications next week. All right?"

"All right," I whispered, taking my cup to the booth in the back. Taylor's booth.

As I stared down at the vanilla ice cream, the purple sprinkles slowly bleeding into its pearly whiteness, I narrowed my eyes.

What am I missing? I thought to myself, popping a spoonful into my mouth. *I've gone over everything a thousand times, and yet, I still feel blocked.*

My mind drifted over to Clara, as it usually did during my sessions at the ice cream shop. I thought of her heart-shaped face and beautiful blue eyes, a smile finding its way onto my face. I winced as her expression morphed into the pain she'd worn on November 15th. I'd taken care of her; nursed her wounds, even slept on the couch one night to make sure she was safe. Mr. And Mrs. Lawson didn't mind – they didn't seem to pay much attention to anything since Taylor's disappearance.

148

I thought about my parents. They weren't very present, but, when they were, I felt comfortable talking to them about anything. *That's what every kid wants, right?* I thought. *A healthy, happy relationship with their family.* My parents weren't unhappy – their marriage was good, and they were very much in love – everything was fine.

Still, the block. Sitting right in my chest, something deep and intricate, *just* out of my reach. It followed me in my car, at school, when I went to bed at night and when I woke up in the morning. It was always there, a ghost shadowing my everyday life.

I took another bite of my ice cream.

Is it the sense of unpredictability? I wondered. *My entire routine has been thrown off. Maybe I need to establish some normalcy – get back to work, football, all that.*

But I knew that wasn't it. Football, the ice cream shop – it was all the same, and it wasn't what I was looking for.

Maybe I'm just imagining it, I reasoned, eating some more. *Maybe it's not even there.*

I dropped my spoon in my cup and ran my hand along the length of my chest, my fingertips traveling over the soft cotton of my tee. There were no marks, no bumps or visible scarring, just a block deep in my ribcage, like a brick or a chunk of cement.

It made it hard to breathe, too. Even if it wasn't necessarily physical, it still felt like a weight, crushing my lungs and sucking the air out of my throat. It was exhausting – keeping up with this frustratingly invisible force – and I knew I had to deal with it before I could move on.

It could be disappointment. Joe had taken over the position as head captain, demoting me to co-captain. It made sense – he was a superior player, and he never skipped practices, but it still felt like a slap in the face. How would it look on my resume? Like Joe said, things were getting more competitive, and even the slightest hitch could be disastrous.

It wasn't football.

I took another bite.

It's not stress over Clara, I deduced. *If anything, she's a lot less to handle than Taylor. She's been good, and funny, and kind – she's honest, even if she keeps things to herself. It's refreshing.*

Scratch Clara off the list, which was distinctly narrowing. Not Clara, not football, not my parents, not the newly-found turmoil my life has been thrown into.

Is it Taylor?

The questions I'd been avoiding bubbled up to the surface. *Is she safe? Where is she? Will I ever see her again?* It was hard to think about, but not impossible. Taylor was someone that would stay with me for a long time – I knew that for certain – but she'd left. I missed her smile, and her jokes, and her purple hair, but I didn't miss her.

There was one bite left in my cup.

I sat back, glancing over my shoulder at where Sara was wiping down the counters. I looked around at the glass windows and dim lighting, the cups and cones stacked up near the register and behind the tips jar. I listened to the quiet rush of a car passing by, and the whir of the freezers that kept the ice cream cold. I noticed the door to the back room was slightly open, revealing a sliver of Sara's messy desk, piled high with papers.

She had work to do, and it wasn't fair of me to make her take over my duties out of pity. I'd ask for my job back soon, but, for now...

I stood and threw away my cup, lingering disappointedly by the door. Another day, zero progress made. And the block in my chest was just as prominent as ever, spreading all the way up to my shoulders and weighing my arms down. I reached up and rubbed the back of my neck, closing my eyes as I felt warmth spread down my spine.

Right then, it hit me.

I slowly sat back down at my table, staring at a drop of spilled ice cream on the shiny wood. Tears began to bubble up into my eyes as the realization that had been in front of me all along settled in, shooting up and down my body like an icy shiver.

I've forgotten to take care of myself.

I was so busy worried about other people and other things, I'd forgotten to let myself feel. Forgotten to grieve over Taylor, to panic over the future, to simply be. I'd shoved everything down until it'd accumulated into the block in my chest, waiting to be released. And now, I wasn't sure if I could handle it all by myself.

With glossy eyes, I ran out of the ice cream shop.

***

It took everything I had to hold it in on the drive to Clara's. I focused intently on the road, my knuckles tight around the wheel as I bit the inside of my cheek. I blinked back the tears and breathed deeply, forcing myself to calm down. To hold it in for just a few minutes, until I pulled into the Lawson's driveway.

Please let it be Clara, I begged silently, raising my hand to knock on the door.

It swung inward before my fist could connect with the wood, revealing Clara in a hoodie and leggings, her hair ruffled and her eyes red. She'd been sleeping.

It all burst out.

I started crying. Huge, enormous sobs racked my shoulders and buckled my knees, pouring out through my eyes and my mouth as I unleashed it all. The stress, the worries, the gratitude I had for Clara and her instincts, her quiet compliance as she led me to the couch and laid me down onto the soft leather.

Clara's small fingers pushed my hair out of my face as I curled in on myself, my cries echoing throughout the empty house. And Clara, kneeling beside me as she looked on with soft eyes and a gentle touch, there for me. More there for me than Taylor had been during our entire relationship. More there for me than my absent parents had been my entire life. More there for me than football, than the ice cream shop, than anything had ever been before.

Clara was there for me when I unblocked myself.

I'll never forget that.

<u>sunset</u>

When I next awoke, my eyes were swollen shut.

"Wh – I can't see!" I cried, grabbing at my face.

"Aaron!" Clara's voice sounded from nearby, followed by the pressure of her hands on my shoulders. "Aaron, you're okay!"

"But I can't–"

"I'm going to get you some ice," she whispered soothingly, easing me back down against the soft leather. "Try not to freak out, okay?"

I sucked in a deep, calming breath. "Okay," I murmured, relaxing as I felt her weight lift off. Running my hands over the pillow behind me, I realized it was rough and embroidered, the pattern faintly impressed on the outside of my cheek.

"Here, this should help," Clara said, pressing a cold pack against my face. I hissed through my teeth, but, gradually, the red-hot pain around my eyes began to subside.

"It's working," I sighed, lowering the pack to blink feebly. "Thank you."

"Are you okay?" She asked quietly. "When you showed up here last night, I wasn't sure if–"

"Oh... oh, God." I sat forward and pressed my palms to my eyes, the events of the previous night finally returning. "I'm so sorry. I wasn't sure where else to go, since I didn't think I could handle being in an empty house–"

153

"I'm glad you came." I glanced up, and found her smiling at me, her tired blue eyes swimming with something identifiable.

In that moment, the only thing I wanted to do was stay right there, wrapped up on Clara's couch with an ice pack, but I knew I couldn't afford to ignore my responsibilities forever. "I'm missing football practice... I should go." My eyes fell on the nest of blankets on the floor beside the couch as I grabbed my shoes, pulling them on one by one.

"Are you sure?" Clara asked, eyeing me cautiously. "You want me to drive you?"

I paused. "Actually," I said, a smile sneaking up my face. "That'd be great."

***

"Crap, I'm a half hour late," I sighed, buckling in my seatbelt as Clara sped down the road.

"Normally I drive like an old lady, but I'll make an exception," Clara said, flooring the gas pedal. I cried out as my head slammed back against my seat, the small black car careening around the corner dangerously fast.

"Maybe you can find a healthy medium between 'old lady' and 'race car driver'!" I screamed, laughing as we spun around another corner. Clara burst out into giggles as she was thrown against the door, finally halting the car by the side of the road.

"Okay, breathing," she sighed, still grinning. "Let's get you to that stadium."

When we arrived at the practice, my teammates had already moved on from warmups to drills. "Thanks for the ride," I told Clara, grabbing my duffel bag out of the backseat of the car. "I'll call you."

"Hang on a second!" Clara cried, jumping out of the car. I watched her incredulously as she shouldered her bag and marched right up to me. "I'm gonna watch your practice."

"It's gonna go for another three hours," I said, eyeing her.

"I know. I have my journal, and a fully-charged phone." She linked her arm with mine, grinning brightly. "Let's do this, Parker."

Chuckling, I lead her towards the entrance to the field, where I found Joe leaning against the chain-linked fence.

"Joe," I said, detaching myself from Clara to head over to the tall boy. "Shouldn't you be with the others?"

"I figured I'd come meet you," he said, turning his attention to Clara. He nodded, and she paused, the smile instantly slipping from her face.

Confused, I watched as she slowed her steps, sliding around Joe as they kept their gazes locked.

"Do you guys... know each other?" I asked.

Joe broke the stare. "No," he said. "Get on out to the field, *partner*."

Not buying his act, I glanced at Clara one last time before heading over to the benches, watching the girl's dusty hair head up into the bleachers.

"Glad you decided to grace us with your presence, Parker," Coach Caputo growled into my ear, slapping me on the back as I began to fill my water bottle. For whatever reason, I welcomed the snide, and found myself smiling as I headed out onto the field.

***

Hours later, after practice, I climbed up into the stands to sit with Clara.

"You must be exhausted," she sympathized, setting down her journal to pat my hand. "You need more water?"

"My water's fine, thanks," I laughed, then sighed. "I am tired. But it gave me something to do, you know?"

"Yeah." Clara turned her eyes out in front of us. "Beautiful sunset."

"It really is," I agreed, my eyes trailing over the mesh of colors snaking across the sky. When I glanced over at Clara, I found her frowning down at her book. "What's the matter?"

"It's just..." She forced out a sad smile, hugging her arms around her. "I can't write it, you know? Words are my thing, and I just... I could never capture it. Not something like that."

My eyes flickered back to the sunset for a brief moment. "You can try," I encouraged her. "You're already amazing, and you'll only get better with practice."

"There are just some things words can't describe." She stood. "Come on, let's go back to my place. We can order takeout; whatever kind you want."

"I could *really* go for some Chinese right now."

"Chinese it is, then."

She smiled at me, stepping down the bleachers as I gathered my gear. I pushed my hair out of my face as I watched her go.

She's right, I thought to myself. *There are some things words simply can't capture.*

I wasn't thinking about the sunset.

nap

The next morning, I awoke to a text from Clara.

From Clara, 4:04 AM: do you have Taylor's phone?

I frowned down at the screen, taking time to carefully plan my response.

To Clara, 9:09 AM: No, the police confiscated it. They found it in a trash can in the stadium, remember?

She responded immediately.

From Clara, 9:09 AM: right

Are you all right?

fine

I'm coming over.

that's fine, too

***

"Mom and dad were talking about her yesterday. I guess I just had a brain fart." Clara was slowly braiding her hair, sitting cross-legged across from me on the carpet of her living room.

"It was 4 AM," I reminded her. "How are you even awake right now?"

"I stayed up writing." She shrugged. "It's almost winter break, and I don't do homework. What else am I supposed to work on?"

"Speaking of which, I noticed you didn't have a Christmas tree," I said. "Are you Jewish?"

"No, but I'm not sure if we'll have a Christmas this year." She shrugged. "With everything that's happened, I understand."

My heart ached. "That's no fun. You should come celebrate with my family."

"Are you going to church?"

"No, b–"

"Would you like to?"

I cocked my head at her. "You want to go to church?"

"I don't go that often." She looked down at her lap. "Recently, though, I've been attending a lot more services. Praying for her, you know."

I knew. "Yeah, we can go to church."

She smiled tiredly. "I should go take a nap. What else are you up to today?"

"Not sure," I said, following her to her room. "You want me to get out of here?"

"No, stay," Clara said quickly, glancing at me over her shoulder. "I don't – I can't fall asleep in an empty house."

So she hadn't just been writing. "Where are your parents?"

Clara said nothing, busying herself with slipping beneath the thick comforter draped over her bed. She fluffed her pillows and smoothed down wrinkles, all the while ignoring the question hanging in the air like a lead weight.

"I'll stay," I told her, kneeling beside the bed to take her hand. "You sleep."

She nodded beneath her hair, and I suddenly realized how tired she looked. She'd been through enough for several lifetimes, and I decided that the least I could do for her was to hold her hand while she fell asleep.

Which actually took surprisingly long. Ten minutes later, I was still waiting for her breathing to become even, but she kept getting a crease in her brow, and I could only wonder what was going on inside that mind of hers.

Clara took so long to fall asleep, I felt my eyelids drooping involuntarily, my body sagging against the nightstand next to her bed.

I slept holding her hand, feeling more comfortable on the floor of her bedroom than I had in a long, long time.

***

Bzzt.

My eyelids fluttered open, immediately registering the uncomfortable way my legs were curled up beneath me, all feeling lost below my knees.

Biting down on my lip to keep from groaning, I slowly eased out my joints, slipping my hand out of Clara's and massaging the sore muscles. My cheek was dented from the wood of her nightstand, and my neck was absolutely killing me, but it somehow felt worth it.

I glanced up to see it was still light outside, so I slowly climbed to my feet and looked over at Clara one last time.

She was beautiful.

With her hair falling around crazily, she looked like something straight out of a cartoon. Her lips were parted and her arms were spread wide, completely vulnerable and open. I realized then how closed off she always was, even to me. But right then, the tension in her shoulders was gone, along with her stiff joints and permanent frown. There, sleeping like she was, Clara was more herself than I'd ever seen her be, and I loved that.

As I quietly left the room, my resolve to figure out Clara Lawson solidified, excitement hammering at my heart at the thought of the future.

closet

Clara was sweating.

She was sitting across from me with her eyes wider than I'd ever seen them before, her face devoid of all color as she glanced around nervously. All I could think about was that intense blue gaze.

A few hours earlier, I'd met up with her before school in the school lobby, helping her carry her books to her first class.

"So, I'll see you at lunch?" I said to her, setting the mound of textbooks down on her usual desk in the back.

"Actually, about that," she began, and I tilted my head at her, waiting for her to go on. "I was thinking I could eat lunch with you today."

I blinked. "You eat lunch with me every day, Clara."

"No." She grinned. "I mean... I hate dragging you away from your friends. It's gotta be getting boring, sitting alone with me."

"It's not boring," I protested, but she held her hand up to silence me.

"I wanna eat with you, and your friends." She bounced on her heels, anxiety evidently overtaking her. "The football... squad, or whatever you call it."

I laughed. "*You* want to eat lunch with *my* friends?"

"Yeah... if that's okay." She glanced up at me timidly, and I wrinkled my nose.

"Of course it's okay," I said. "We'll just meet in our usual spot, and I'll take you to them. Okay?"

"Okay."

A pause. "Are you gonna freak out?"

"I figured the best way to confront my anxiety is to face it head on." She hugged her arms around her. "What's more anxiety-provoking than sitting in the midst of a bunch of talented guys?"

"*Talented.*" I snorted. "This kid named Lance was trying to see if he could fart into his water bottle last practice."

"EW!" Clara slapped my arm, struggling to suppress a laugh. "You know what I mean! Now, get out of here. The bell's about to ring."

"Tired of me already?" I joked, heading for the door.

"Never. I'll see you at lunch!"

Now, it was lunch.

Clara looked scared out of her mind. The other guys at the table were eyeing her warily, evidently suspicious of the newcomer. It didn't help that some of my teammates' girlfriends were giving her nasty looks, something both Clara and I had completely forgotten to factor in.

I looked down at my lap, sneakily sending out a text.

U need me 2 help you join the conversation?

Clara's phone buzzed, and she eyed it below the table.

you don't need to text me. im right here.

But you texted me back.

She looked up and glared at me, and I grinned.

fine. yes. help pls.

I looked up, scanning around the group for a potential candidate.

"Hey, George," I called to the big-looking boy at the end of the table. His head snapped up.

"Sup?" He asked.

"You're into writing, right?" I asked. "Clara writes, too."

George's pudgy face lit up. "Really?" He asked. "That's awesome!"

"So do you, like, write stories?" A bored-looking redhead by the name of Cheyenne asked, smacking her gum as she stared condescendingly at Clara. My eyes narrowed.

"Yeah, kind of," Clara peeped, then cleared her throat. "Some poetry, too, sometimes."

"Can we, like, read some of your stuff?" Cheyenne asked, pulling a nail filer out of her purse.

"Oh, um–" Clara began, glancing at me pleadingly. I took the signal and interrupted.

"I'm not sure if–" I began, but was cut off.

"Yeah, let's hear," a girl named Hannah chirped. "Big writer! Are you published?"

"I – I–" Clara sputtered.

Suddenly, all the girls were talking over themselves, eager to pick Clara apart like vultures. As a football player, I'd grown up around popular girls all my life, and recognized the signs of them preying.

"I'm gonna head to the lunch line," I announced, standing up suddenly. "Clara, come with me?"

She nodded quickly, hiding her beet red face, and swung her legs over the bench to meet me as I rounded the table.

"Grab my hand," I whispered into her ear, brushing my fingers with hers as we began to walk. "Squeeze it. Don't let go."

Clara quickly locked her fingers in mine, keeping her head low as I steered her out of the cafeteria. Searching around frantically, I finally spied a janitor's closet at the end of the hallway, and quickly ushered her small form into it.

I shut the door behind us, plunging the small space into darkness, and quickly flicked on the single light hanging from the ceiling. Satisfied, I returned my attention to Clara.

She was hyperventilating.

"Hey, breathe," I whispered, bending down in front of her as I took her hand. "Breathe, okay? Steadily, like me."

"I just — the girls — they wanted — I don't — I can't—" Clara stuttered, her shoulders shaking violently. Panic began to bubble up in my throat as I cursed myself. *You should have prepared for this.*

Suddenly, I had an idea.

"Clara," I whispered soothingly, rubbing the back of her hand. "Did I ever tell you about the time I went camping?"

A few frantic breaths. "No," she panted.

"It was with my dad during one of his rare breaks. As soon as he got off his shift at the hospital, we packed up and headed for the mountains, and we backpacked up along some beautiful streams and through these wonderful, old forests." I smiled fondly. "The forest was humid and itchy, but I loved looking up and seeing the starlight through the trees. I felt like I was in a movie."

Clara swallowed, still frightened.

"On the last day, we were hiking up this hill when I tripped and cut my hand open on a rock." I winced, remembering the pain. "It was awful. There was blood everywhere, and I was screaming, and I thought to myself, *there's no one around for miles. There's no one around to save me.*"

"This is supposed to be *helping*?!" Clara demanded, and I quickly grabbed her other hand.

"Listen," I whispered. "There was no one around, but there was my dad, the best surgeon in all of Texas. He remained calm, sitting me down on a rock and talking me through it, keeping me distracted as he cleaned and stitched up my hand." I looked down at my feet. "He was so brave that day. He saved me."

Finally, Clara began to calm down, squeezing my hand tightly in her grip.

"*You* keep saving everyone," she murmured. "Taylor, me, your parents... even yourself. You're constantly being the hero, and you don't ever ask for anything in return."

My heart leapt in my throat.

Tears brimmed in Clara's eyes, and I blinked, realizing I'd only seen her cry one other time, on the day of the Paris attacks.

"I'm so sorry," she whispered. "I wish I wasn't me. I wish it more than anything in the world."

She raised her brilliant blue gaze to the door, her lower lip trembling.

I tilted her chin up to face me. "I'm glad you are you."

I'd planned to kiss Clara Lawson for a long, long time. I don't remember when I made the decision, but when I did, I began planning out how to go about it, mapping out long lists of settings and romantic settings. I certainly didn't expect, or want, our first kiss to be in a dusty old janitor's closet.

There was nothing special about that kiss. Nothing special about the outfits we were wearing, or the place we were in; in fact, it all felt so completely normal that I almost didn't register it was happening. It was a normal, everyday kiss.

The only thing special about that kiss was that I couldn't stand to not be kissing Clara Lawson for another moment. Every single fiber of my being ached for her until all my plans evaporated into thin air.

And then we were kissing.

curb

The next day after practice, I found Joe and Clara talking.

"Hey, what's going on here?" I said, sliding up to where they were standing. Clara was wearing a big hoodie over black leggings, her hair tied back into two braids. She looked adorable, but I didn't say so.

"I was just telling Clara about how well you've been doing," Joe said idly.

"Aaron–" Clara began, but Joe cut her off.

"I should really get going." He began to back away. "You have my number?"

"Yeah," Clara murmured, and my brows drew together. I watched Joe walk off before turning to Clara.

"What's really going on?" I asked her, taking her hand. "It's been a day, Clara."

"I know it's been a day." Her jaw clenched. "Don't you think I know it's been a day?"

"Sorry, I–" I faltered, uncertain of where the sudden hostility had come from. "Are you okay?"

"Taylor and I have lived here our whole lives." She turned and crossed her arms across her chest, staring right at Joe, where he was getting into his car.

"Yeah?" I asked. "I'm not sure I follow–"

"Joe hasn't."

I couldn't help but grin. "You're being all cryptic."

"When he first came to the house, I didn't like him."

My grin vanished. "What?" I asked. "Joe's been to your house? When?"

"He was an outsider. He used to go to Frawley, you know that? Our biggest rival. Joe's from there."

My mouth bobbed open and closed like a fish.

"Taylor was angry." Clara sank down onto the curb, hugging her legs to her chest. "Someone at this school had cheated on her. A football player. She wanted to get back at him."

I sat back down next to her, running my hands through my hair.

"So she and Joe dated. For a year and a half, they dated."

"They... they..." I sputtered, my mind racing. I thought back to Joe, his eyes scanning the bleachers for Taylor, referring to her when we talked...

"One day it just ended." Clara swallowed heavily. "I'd grown to like him. Tolerate him, at least. He was always around, and that was okay. I like routine, you know."

"What happened?" I asked dumbly.

"I'm not sure." Clara leaned into me, her shoulder pressing into my side. "I read through their text messages. Taylor asked him to meet her

170

for coffee, and then they never texted again. I don't know what happened in that coffee shop, and, after Taylor disappeared, I thought to myself, *now I never will.*"

I sat back. "You were asking Joe about her."

"No." She raised her eyes to mine, telling the truth. Clara always told the truth. "He came up to me."

"And?"

"He said that, if I ever saw her, to say hello for him."

A pause. "When did Taylor and Joe break up?"

"On the day she went for coffee, Taylor came home, grabbed her purse, and told me we were going for ice cream."

My heart stopped. "No."

"And that's where she met you."

I pushed myself to my feet, staggering down the sidewalk.

"Aaron, wait." Clara hurried up to me and snaked her fingers through mine. "Tell me what you're thinking."

I stopped, sucking in deep breaths of air. Clara looked up into my face, her blue eyes wide with concern, and my expression immediately softened.

"I'm thinking," I began, stepping closer to her, "about how beautiful you look right now."

And then I kissed her again.

church

It was Christmas Eve.

A week had passed since Clara and I had kissed for the second time, and six days since we'd last spoken. Since then, I'd come to accept the idea of Joe being Taylor's ex. After all, it was in the past. Taylor was gone, Joe and I were teammates, and everything was fine.

I was sitting on the couch in my living room, staring up at the glimmering lights of the Christmas tree in front of me. I'd done a beautiful job, and dad had been home long enough to perform the ceremonial crowning of the star. Now, both of my parents were in the house, fixing themselves hot cocoa and getting everything ready for the next day. I knew they'd be pulled into a surgery soon – the holidays were one of the busiest times of the year – so I was just trying to enjoy the sense of their presence in the household, listening to the small sounds of life trickling out of the other rooms.

Mom hurried out and pulled her coat off of the rack. "Dinner's in the fridge," she murmured. "We'll be home to put out the presents tonight."

"Love you," I said absentmindedly, keeping my gaze fixed in front of me. "Don't work too hard."

She paused in the doorway, and I glanced over to find her grinning brilliantly.

"I'm so proud of you, Aaron," she whispered, not waiting for my reply before shutting the door behind her.

Although the house felt a little emptier, warmth bloomed in my chest.

***

I didn't text Clara, but somehow, I knew she'd be at the church. Partially because it was Christmas Eve, and partially because it just felt so *right*. I walked there, my breath filtering out in wisps of fog, dressed in a heavy-duty jacket and beanie. The cold wouldn't last much longer, and, although I preferred the sweltering heat of summer, I decided to savor the chilly weather while it lasted.

As I came upon the grounds, I noticed the way the stained-glass windows of the church were brilliantly reflecting light out onto the street, casting shadows of color across the monochromatic asphalt. I smiled softly to myself as I stepped up to the grand doors, my gloved hand hovering over the knob for a good half minute.

Finally, I pulled the door open, peering inside to find the rows of rows of empty pews leading to the altar. Dozens of lit candles were scattered across the sacred space, providing a dim, yet serene, atmosphere.

And there was Clara, the sole leftover from Christmas mass, sitting alone in the second row of seats. I recognized her wavy brown hair immediately, and the gray beanie hugged around her head.

She knew I was there – my steps echoed loudly around the cavernous walls as I walked down the aisle – but she didn't turn around. As I approached, I discovered she was bent over her lap, her hands pressed together in prayer.

I slipped into the pew behind her, and was just about to lean forward to touch her neck when she spoke.

"God, I need you to hear me," she whispered, her shoulders trembling. I pulled back, knowing I shouldn't listen in on such a private conversation, but curiosity got the best of me. "I know you don't owe Taylor anything – she's done enough damage herself – but you owe *me*.

174

You *owe me*, God. After what you put me through—" she paused, sucking in a shuddering breath, "—I lost my faith in you. Mom kept telling me, 'God has a plan. Please come to church.' But I just couldn't bring myself to. I thought, what kind of a God allows *that* to happen?"

I blinked, my lips parting in wonder.

"I am a simple person, God," Clara whispered. "I am a simple person, but Taylor is not. Taylor is a tangled mess of lies and craziness and who knows what else, and she needs help. She needs someone to smooth out those wrinkles, to guide her back to shaping the potential she's always had within her. She could've been a doctor. Or a lawyer. Or the goddamn president, I don't know." A pause. "It's not too late for her. I know it, and you know it. So please, God. This is me cashing in my favor."

I waited, breathless with apprehension.

"Please just take care of her." There was sadness in Clara's voice. "Please... show me a sign, God. Show me that you'll take care of her."

Now it was my turn to speak. "Hey," I whispered, and Clara whirled around, her wide eyes landing on where I was sitting.

After a moment, she turned back around, and I could see the smile on her face.

"Thank you," she whispered.

***

Clara and I sat in the church for a long while, our knees touching as we stared up at the altar in wonder.

She was the first to speak. "You're amazing," she whispered, and I glanced at her, burying my hands deeper into my jacket pockets.

"So are you," I said.

"You're amazing, and..." She tucked a strand of hair behind her ear, a small frown tugging at her lips, "...it just feels... wrong. Being with you, after Taylor, and everything you two had..."

"I know," I told her, sighing. "I feel the same way. But I just can't feel guilty when every time I'm with you it feels like my entire world is on fire."

Clara blinked, slowly raising her eyes to mine.

"What Taylor and I had was special," I went on, fixing my gaze on the glimmering wooden cross hanging from the ceiling, "and she's someone I still miss every day. I'll miss her for a long time, and I'll miss everything we had." I smiled tensely. "But, in the aftermath, looking back on it all, I realized it was never meant to last. The truth was bound to come out, and I just can't love someone who endangers her life; other people's lives, too." I closed my eyes as I thought of Devon. He'd quit the football team and checked himself into rehab, and I knew Taylor had done that to him. "Someone reckless, and irresponsible, and just overall–"

"Is this really the place for this?" Clara squeaked, and my expression softened.

"You're a healer, Clara," I said, my hand itching to hold hers. "You do nothing but love and support people, and now I want to love and support you." I ran my hands through my hair. "And, yeah, we'll take it slow. We'll respect Taylor and everything that happened over the past few months, but we'll be *moving forward*. That's the most important thing."

Clara leaned into my shoulder, and my heart leapt into my chest. "Forward, huh?" She asked quietly.

I nodded. "Forward," I said.

christmas

On Christmas Day, Clara and I met up in a Jewish deli (the only place that was open) to exchange our gifts.

"Hot chocolate for me, please," she said to the barista. I grinned at her.

"You know, it's a little embarrassing that you don't get coffee at a coffee shop," I teased.

She flushed. "Could you *not*?! It was hard enough ordering for myself, cut me some slack!"

"Okay, okay." I held my hands up in a sign of peace. We got our drinks and headed to a table, where I gestured at her. "Ladies first."

She went tense. "I'm not sure if you'll like it," she said shyly, dropping her gaze to her lap.

"Well, it's from you, so that automatically gives it a boost." I narrowed my eyes at her. "It's not a sweater, or something, is it?"

She laughed. "No, it's not," she chuckled. "It's just... you go first. Please?"

"Clara–"

"Pretty please?" She batted her eyelashes at me.

"Don't you do that," I chuckled, wrinkling my nose at her. "You know I can't resist the big eyes."

"I'm not sure what you're talking about." Clara propped her face up with her hands, jutting out her lower lip. "This is my normal face."

"Is not!" I cried, then caved. "Fine. Just a heads up, I'm terrible at wrapping presents."

"It's what's on the *inside* that counts," Clara teased, drawing a heart on the back of my hand with her finger as I reached into my backpack. I pulled out her gift, messily wrapped in light blue paper. "Eeee! I'm so excited!" Clara squealed, grabbing my gift and tearing into the paper. I smirked as she unraveled the package within, noting the way her shoulders hiked up with anticipation.

"Do you like it?" I asked, folding my arms across my chest.

"*No.*"

My grin vanished. "What?"

"I meant... you did *not*." Her wide eyes returned to my face, and I laughed. "Aaron..."

"Well?"

"They're beautiful." She clutched the package of German mechanical pencils to her chest, sucking in deep breaths of air. "I love them."

"There's more," I told her, pointing at the package.

Clara gasped. "A gift card for the ice cream shop!!"

"I start work again tomorrow," I told her, leaning over the table to wrap her into a hug. "Merry Christmas."

"Merry Christmas," Clara chirped, planting a kiss on my cheek as I pulled away. "Dammit... I should have gone first."

"You're too dramatic," I said. "I'm sure I'll love it."

"I don't know." Her brows furrowed together, and her lips tightened into a line. For a moment, she seemed like she was retreating into herself, reverting into the closed-off Clara that I'd come to hate.

"Hey," I told her, reaching out to put my hand on hers. "You don't have to give it to me. I'm fine."

"No, that's probably worse," Clara sighed, a small smile appearing on her face as she reached into her messenger bag. "It's just... anxiety."

"You have nothing to be anxious about," I told her. "You know... you know I love you, right?"

Her head snapped up, a wide smile slowly spreading across her face.

"I love you, too," she said, feeding strength off of the words. "Okay. Here it is."

She pulled out a shiny rectangular package with a bow, flawlessly wrapped, naturally. She watched nervously as I accepted it from her hands.

I unfolded back the perfect creases, my heart in my throat as I pulled out her present.

"It's not much," Clara interjected, her voice breaking. "Those expensive pencils... God, am I a terrible girlfriend? I've never actually been someone's girlfriend before, so I think I have a lot to–"

"Clara," I whispered, and she gripped onto the edge of the table with white knuckles.

"Do you hate it?" She asked.

"No," I whispered, running my hands over the cover of the notebook. "It's just... I remember you talking about this. This is the first notebook you ever kept. I can't take this."

"Well, of course not." She scoffed. "It's yours to *borrow*. I'll need it back, eventually – I'm thinking about typing it all up. Into a real book, you know?"

"That sounds great," I told her, grinning supportively.

She bit her lower lip. "It seemed a lot bigger to me, in my head," she murmured, running her hands through her hair. "It's just... it's my way of opening up to you, you know? Everything you need to know about me is in those pages." She pointed with a shaky finger. "Including..."

My mouth dropped open.

"Including the '*incident*'," I finished.

the incident

I never liked writing.

I guess things change.

I still don't necessarily *like* writing, though. After all, I'm basically being forced to do this – I can feel Dr. Charleston's eyes on the back of my neck. I don't like him, either. He keeps referring to me as a 'victim'. *You were the victim of something horrible, Clara.*

I'm not a victim. I'm a survivor.

Dr. Charleston also keeps trying to get me to talk about my feelings. *How do you feel about this, Clara? What emotion comes to mind when I say that, Clara?* And then he gets this little crease in his brow when I always answer with the same thing:

Nothing. I feel nothing.

I don't have trigger words. I don't have a loss of appetite. I don't even have nightmares. Dr. Charleston says that if I keep suppressing everything, it will eventually all bubble up into something unpredictable. Violent, maybe. So, by all means, I'm down for treatment. I'm down to sit in this office every day at four o'clock, talking it all through over and over again. But, Dr. Charleston told me to be honest, and I honestly feel nothing. If I'm suppressing anything, it's completely unintentional.

I guess that's why he recommended daily sessions to my parents; why I'm sitting here on a Friday afternoon when everyone my age is out with their friends. I heard there's a new movie, and I'd like to go see it. Mom won't let me out of the house, though.

When I told Dr. Charlestown that I found this notebook, he told me to write in it. *Writing is easier than talking.* He told me to put down anything and everything that comes to mind. My hands are small, and they cramp easily, so I'm not sure they'll make it through the entire session. I'll try, though.

Dr. Charleston will be reading this, so I guess I should be addressing him directly, but it seems wrong. I think I should tell it like a story, because that's what it feels like. Beginning, middle, and end.

So I'll start from the beginning.

Obviously, it was at Calvin's. I was there because it was my favorite pizza place, and now it will never open again. I'll never get to taste Calvin's double-cheese-deluxe pizza ever again.

I was sitting at my usual table in the corner. I wasn't shy, but I liked to read when I went to Calvin's, and it was quiet over there. I could see the entire restaurant from my chair; that night, it was the dinner 'rush', which consisted of Calvin's twenty regulars (including me) and a few newcomers looking for a bite to eat.

Seventeen people, to be exact.

I had my pizza and my book, and I was getting grease all over the pages, so I wiped my hands off with a napkin and began dabbing at the paper. That's when the three men came in.

I didn't look up. I knew they were there, because a little bell dinged over the front door whenever someone entered, and I heard the soft *click* as they locked the door, but that part didn't register until later. I was too focused on salvaging my greasy book to notice the enormous guns they were holding.

I only looked up when they started shooting, which was a few seconds after their arrival, and I remember thinking that they looked like Navy Seals. The good guys, not the bad guys.

It was loud. *So* loud. So loud I could barely think, barely move, barely breathe. It felt like the air was splitting open all around me.

7:15. I read in the newspaper that that's the time the first gunshot was heard. The men shot the people by the door first, three women waiting to be seated.

Then the shooters took their time reloading, and the deafening noise stopped for about thirty seconds. My hand was hovering above the page of my book, clutching a balled-up napkin between my fingers. Calvin was standing behind the counter, wearing his aquamarine apron, and nobody moved. Everyone was so in shock, we all just watched as the men loaded their bullets and slowly turned around.

When they started firing at us again, everyone leapt into action. I dropped beneath the table as a reflex, spilling my drink in the process. My legs were curled up beneath the edge of the table, and I felt cold water drip down and seep into my pants, but I was too scared to move. There was a tablecloth draped over the table, so I could only just barely see, but I watched the men's boots as they walked. Every single one of their steps was precise and coordinated, not a falter in their path. They walked calmly, as if they were merely taking a stroll, and said nothing as they murdered everyone.

After a minute, the gunshots stopped, and I could hear a woman screaming. A toddler was crying somewhere near the front of the restaurant, too, and I shoved my fist into my mouth to keep from weeping.

I heard the clinking as the men reloaded, and dared to peek my head out from beneath the table. I looked at the attackers first; they wore body armor, and had utility belts stuffed with weapons. They also had more gun holsters than I'd ever seen, and I remember the realization hitting me right then: *they're going to shoot all of us.*

Next, I looked at the restaurant. The eggshell-colored plaster was splattered with maroon, lining the walls like abstract paintings. Pools and pools of blood were spreading over the tile floors, and then there were the bodies. 'Dead' doesn't even begin to describe them – it looked like they were *shredded*, their skin hanging off bones by threads. The men had made sure to fill each and every victim with multiple bullets; it was why over half of us were still alive.

I spotted a group of survivors huddled under a table like I was, and I thought to myself, *it's stupid to hide. They'll find you.* I bit down hard on my knuckles as I watched people scramble for the front door, smearing their hands with the blood that stained the windowless walls. I realized why the men had shot the women by the door first, because their corpses were blocking the way. Even in a frenzy, people were too scared to get close. If they wanted to break the door down, they'd have to move the bodies first.

The back door was also locked. I looked at where a man with sandy-brown hair was struggling with the door, tears streaming down his cheeks as he jiggled the knob furiously. The attackers noticed him, too. As soon as they reloaded, he was the first person they shot.

Since my table was in the corner by the back door, the man fell right nearby, blood streaming down between his lifeless eyes. I scooted away and curled my legs up to my chest, listening to the gunshots ringing on and on.

The men didn't see where I was hiding, so they killed everyone near the back of the shop, then returned their focus towards the bulk of survivors at the front. That's when I made the move from my table to the counter, where I forgot Calvin would be lying. It took everything I had not to scream as I stepped over his body, crouching over his legs in order to peer over the countertop. At first, all three men had shot one person at a time, but then they branched out, each firing in different directions. Bodies dropped to the floor with sickening *thuds*, and, when the shots stopped for a fourth time, I thought everyone was dead.

But then I realized the men found the people hiding under the table, the sobbing of a young child betraying their whereabouts. One of the attackers left the other two, and they watched on as he ripped the tablecloth off to reveal the last survivors.

It was a family. A mother, a father, and a young daughter. The parents shook violently as the man reached into his belt and pulled out a small handgun, slowly raising it to point at them as if he had all the time in the world. He shot them both once, right in their foreheads. The woman's neck bent unnaturally as she fell backwards, the man falling forwards to lay face down.

Then it was just their child, who wasn't screaming, just crying softly as she kept her eyes fixed on the attacker. She couldn't have been more than six or seven years of age, with long brown hair and a dress patterned with purple polka dots, now caked with her parents' fresh blood.

The man took a step back, then turned around and walked back to his partners, and, for a second, I thought they weren't going to shoot her.

But then, as soon as he rejoined them, the other two let loose on their assault rifles, filling her small body with bullets. Everything seemed to go in slow motion – the girl's body convulsed as if she were dancing, her head tilted back, her eyes closed.

That was their final victim. The small girl in the polka dotted dress.

She reminded me of myself.

I dropped back down behind the counter, tears springing to my eyes. I knew it was only a matter of time before they found me – they were now going through the restaurant and shooting the bodies again, making sure they were dead.

This was no robbery. If it was a robbery, they wouldn't have taken so much time killing everyone. They also wouldn't have chosen a place like Calvin's – it's funny, now that I think about it. They never figured out why Calvin's was the target, so I can't help but wonder why they chose there, of all places. There, on that night, the one night I ate at Calvin's. My double-cheese-deluxe pizza was still lying on my table, half-eaten and soaked in water.

I knew there was only one thing I could do. A weak effort, but, since they still hadn't found me, I had to try.

I looked over at Calvin's aquamarine apron, stained black with the blood from the bullets in his chest. I unhooked my fist from my jaw and reached out with shaking fingers, bracing myself for the moment I would put my hands in his blood. Nothing could have prepared me for it, though. I will never be able to describe the feeling of taking my friend's blood and smearing on my face, my arms, my waist... it was as if I was in a horror movie.

Calvin was a big man, so I was almost certain I'd be discovered as I lifted his body. Adrenaline gave me the strength I needed to slip myself underneath his form, my legs sticking out from beneath the other end of his torso. Somehow, the shooters still hadn't found me, so I closed my eyes and went limp, biting down on my tongue to slow my breathing.

You're home in bed, I told myself. *You're home in bed, and it's time to go to sleep. Go to sleep, now.*

I heard one of the attacker's boots squeak on the floor as he rounded the corner. I held my breath as I waited for death to come.

This is it. This is how you die.

For whatever reason, something funny went through my head right then. I'll never forget it, because I found it so odd that, in that moment, as the attacker towered over my body, I thought to myself, *Calvin's double-cheese-deluxe pizza wasn't a bad last meal.*

Then the man fired.

Calvin's thick body stopped the bullets from passing through him and into me, except for one. It went through his side and into mine, slowed enough that I immediately felt it lodge painfully in my hip. My initial instinct was to scream, but I clenched my jaw so tightly stars danced across my eyes, and managed to stay still, waiting for the sound of the man's footsteps to leave.

When I heard the squeal of boots on the bloody floor, I quickly sat up and bared my teeth, letting out a small grunt of agony as I reached to touch where I'd been hit.

It was only then that I opened my eyes.

The attacker hadn't left. He was crouched right beside me, staring into my face through the slits in his mask. His eyes were black, so black I felt myself getting swallowed into them, as if I were staring into the very eyes of death itself. He just sat there, watching me, one hand holding a handgun that rested on his knee.

We stared at each other as the sound of sirens filled the restaurant, as I heard glass shatter and pipes burst, flooding the area behind the counter with bloody water. The man in the mask just kept watching as the policemen, whose armored vehicle had smashed through a wall, shot down one of the attackers, and still kept his eyes on me as his other remaining partner reached over the counter and aimed one gun at him and the other at himself.

He fired both, and I watched the bullet enter through the side of the black-eyed man's head and propel his brains all over the wall, his blood spraying all over where I sat. We were still looking at each other as I felt someone's arms brace beneath mine and lift me up and over the counter, and we didn't break our stare until I'd been dragged into the front of the shop.

From there, I was laid down onto the ground, someone's hands beneath my head for support, and a policeman shone a bright light into my eyes. Everyone was yelling, and there was glass digging into my back, but all I could feel were those coal-black eyes, staring at me from all directions.

I heard someone ask me my name, so I told them.

"Clara," I said, realizing I'd be looking into those eyes for the rest of my life. "Clara Lawson."

I didn't like writing before, but I do now.

Because it feels like that's the only thing that can protect me.

bikini

"Clara, you *have* to."

"No!" She insisted, her voice muffled. "I don't *wanna*."

"Stop it," I laughed.

"Aaron, come *on*. Can't we just go see fireworks like any other couple?"

"No. Besides, we're not just *any* couple." I grinned. "We're Clara and Aaron."

A pause. "Fine. But you have to turn around."

I faced the wall. "I'm not looking."

Clara slowly eased open the door to the dressing room, the hinges creaking loudly as she stepped out into the hallway.

"Okay," she said softly.

I turned to face her, taking in her skinny arms and curvy hips, the bikini top around her chest accentuating features I'd never been able to notice beneath her baggy clothing. She was wearing a black two-piece swimsuit with spaghetti straps, her blue eyes staring up at me in fear as she hugged her arms around her.

"You look great," I told her truthfully, stepping forward to close the distance between us. "I mean it. You really do."

"Who has a swimming party on New Year's, anyway?" Clara grumbled, dropping her gaze. "Levi must be out of his mind."

"Come on—it's a heated pool, and he just wants to celebrate the end of the season. It'll be fun."

My eyes finally landed on the scar near Clara's hipbone, snaking down and around the curve of her upper thigh. My heart ached for her – her own skin was a reminder of that terrible day when she was 13.

"Do you think anyone's going to notice?" Clara asked, catching my gaze. "I can just not go swimming..."

"You're going swimming, and you're going to show off your gorgeous self just the way you are." I pulled her to me, resting my head on top of hers as she sank into my chest. "I love you."

"I love you, too," she said.

***

We arrived at Levi's at 10:00.

"Damn, Parker, looking good!" Joe greeted me, slapping me on the back as Clara and I rounded the corner into the backyard. "This season's done you well, my friend."

He was right. I'd shot up over the past month, gaining pounds of muscle.

"Hey, listen," Joe said, keeping his hand on my shoulder as we walked. "I wanted to talk to you about—"

"Oh, Clara!" Cheyenne cried, springing to her feet as she and her friends caught sight of us. "We've been looking *everywhere* for you! Come on, let's get in the pool!"

A mob of girls swept Clara away, who looked pleadingly over her shoulder as they dragged her towards the poolside.

"I better go help her," I said to Joe, patting him as I stepped away. "Talk later?"

"Yeah," Joe murmured, watching me head off across the yard.

"Aaron!" Levi cried, detaching himself from a throng of players to come greet me by the lawn chairs. "So glad you could make it, man."

"Wouldn't miss it for the world," I told him, smiling politely. "What's the story?"

"Fireworks are set to go off at midnight, burgers are on the grill, and it looks like your girlfriend's about to–" I whirled around just in time to see Clara get pushed into the water, "–yep. I'll see you around?"

"Definitely," I assured him, hurrying towards where Clara was breaking the surface, spluttering and laughing.

"You okay?" I asked her, grabbing her arms, then hauling her out of the pool.

"Y-Yeah," she panted, her eyes shining in the dim light. "That was actually kind of... fun."

"Well, good, because you're about to go again!"

Without any warning, I wrapped my arms around her and tackled her into the pool, the surrounding partygoers applauding in delight. Clara's frantic shriek was cut off by the water enveloping us completely. I let go of her waist and found myself lost in a flurry of bubbles, staring up in wonder as I watched Clara kick up towards the surface, much like an angel ascending to heaven.

After climbing out of the pool, we toweled off and headed towards the food, Clara grabbing the burgers while I was on drinks duty. We met up at the lawn chairs, where I handed Clara a cup of water and cracked open a beer for myself.

"Are you kidding?" She asked incredulously, handing me my food.

"What?" I asked, my eyebrows flying up.

"I'm not a child, Aaron Parker," she teased, snatching my beer out of my hands. "Watch this."

Awestruck, I looked on as she chugged the entire thing, her face contorted in distaste as she downed it completely. When she lowered the can, she was too out of breath to speak, and I was too stunned to move.

"God, that's gross," she coughed, and I burst out laughing.

***

A few hours later, Clara and I were nestled up together as we waited for the clock to tick down to midnight, her damp hair pressing into my chest.

"Thanks for bringing me here," she said, lazily tracing the lines on my stomach with her hand. "I'm glad I came."

"Cheyenne and the others seem to have taken a liking to you," I told her.

"Yeah, it's different." She chewed on her nail.

I stayed quiet, stroking the length of her arm with the pad of my fingertips. "I finished your book."

"What'd you think of it?" She asked, without looking up.

"I think you're the most wonderful person in the entire world, and I'm the luckiest guy ever."

Her cheek grew hot against my skin. "Shut up."

"I love making you blush!"

She giggled as I wrapped my arms around her shoulders, tilting her head up towards the dark sky as chants began to rise up around the crowd.

Ten!

"I'm so glad I met you," Clara whispered.

Eight!

"Here's to a year of great things," I told her, pulling her close.

Five!

Four!

Three!

We were kissing before the timer ticked down, and we kept kissing long after fireworks exploded through the night like the dawn of a new day. It was the perfect moment, with the perfect girl, and I could not have been any happier.

Until someone tapped on my shoulder.

"Hey, man," Joe muttered. "Sorry to interrupt... I just really need to talk to you."

I pulled away from Clara, and she nodded.

"Go," she said. "I'll still be here when you come back."

My heart leapt up into my throat, and I swallowed as I eased myself out from beneath her, following Joe up towards the house. We stepped into the kitchen through the back door, where the tall boy turned to face where I was standing.

"Aaron," Joe began.

"Joe," I said, glancing over at the fireworks rippling across the sky.

"I have a message from Taylor," he said.

And my perfect world shattered.

closure

I met Joe at the park right on time, finding him staring off at the tree line where Taylor had crashed her car. I sidled up next to him, sticking my hands in my pockets as we looked out over the field.

"Any minute now," he said.

"We hope," I said. He nodded, staring down at his feet as silence fell between us.

"You know, I–"

Right then, Joe's cell phone rang in his pocket, and we both went stone-still for the first few chimes, exchanging concerned glances. Joe finally pulled it out of his pocket, then answered.

"Hello?" He asked, then turned to me, unsurprised. "It's for you."

Swallowing heavily, I accepted the phone, watching him start off across the field, giving me my privacy.

"Yeah?" I asked softly.

"Hey," said the smooth, velvety voice on the other line.

"Hey, Taylor," I whispered.

***

"I'm not here to explain myself," Taylor murmured. "We both know what I did – what I'm *doing* – is wrong."

"Why are you here, then?" I asked. "If you're looking for closure—"

"I'm at a pay phone somewhere in Mexico," she interrupted. "I'm going to be traveling down to South America in about an hour."

"Are you alone?" I asked, raising my eyes to the cloudy sky.

"Yeah. I've been sleeping in a car for the past few months, but I have enough cash to keep me going for a while."

I swallowed heavily. "And?"

"And..." She trailed off, sucking in a deep breath.

My mind wandered to all the thousands of things I wanted to say to her in that moment, all the questions I wanted to ask, all the things I'd thought about over the past few months.

"Clara told you about what happened to her, right?" Taylor asked, and I stayed quiet. "Figures. She loves you, and that's good. You two are good for each other."

A pause.

"I think about you every day."

I blinked back sudden tears.

"I'm sorry."

"I know," I said.

"Tell boo I love her."

"I will."

"Talk to her, okay? She needs someone."

"Okay."

She choked back a sob. "She deserved a better sister."

I pressed the palm of my hand to my eye. "It's not too late. You can still come home."

She didn't hesitate. "You know I can't do that."

We stayed quiet for a moment, listening to each other's breathing on the other line. My throat closed with nostalgia.

"She used to sing in the car," Taylor whispered, and a silent tear streamed down my cheek. "She has the most beautiful voice."

I closed my eyes.

"I have to go," she said.

"Be safe," I said, knowing it was enough.

"Goodbye, Aaron."

"Goodbye, Taylor."

We hung up at the same time.

birthday

Clara blew out the candles, smiling brightly as everyone around her applauded. Her hair was tied back into a high ponytail, stray locks spilling down onto her shoulders. She was wearing a beautiful yellow sundress, appropriate for the sweltering heat outside, and she looked spectacular, but, then again, she always did.

Mrs. Lawson kissed the top of her daughter's head, smiling tiredly as she joined hands with a greying Mr. Lawson. The four of us were gathered around the kitchen table, watching as Clara cut into her cake. It was her 17th birthday.

A few months ago, Clara and her parents wouldn't even be in the same room, let alone celebrating a holiday together.

But that was a few months ago.

Time works magic, sometimes.

"That's huge!" I exclaimed, gasping dramatically as Clara handed me my slice.

"Oh, shut up," she scolded lightly, wrinkling her nose. "You're a big boy. You can take it."

"Fine," I sighed resignedly, accepting the plate. "I'll be outside, okay?"

"Be right there," she said distractedly, busy dishing out the other portions. She'd made the cake herself, a 'birthday cake ice cream birthday cake', and it melted deliciously in my mouth as I headed out onto the front porch, parking myself on the bench swing.

"Got my report card," Clara said, and I looked over to see her standing in the doorway, cradling her plate of cake in her hands.

"Oh, yeah?" I asked curiously, patting the seat beside me as she headed across the porch.

"All Bs," she boasted proudly, and I laughed as I noticed a smear of blue frosting on her upper lip.

"Pig," I teased, wiping the glob away with my thumb. "Congratulations. You earned it."

"I did have some help," she said lightly, referencing the dozens of hours of tutoring we'd put in since the New Year. I grinned, snaking my arm around her waist as we looked out over the lawn. I'd gotten a new car for my 18th birthday, and it was parked by the curb, sleek and polished in the glimmering sunlight.

"How's your mom doing?" I asked, popping a forkful of cake into my mouth. It had been almost ten months since Taylor had left, and Mrs. Lawson had recently been struggling with feelings of guilt and regret.

"She's good," Clara said, leaning her head on my shoulder. "You know, this is my first birthday without Taylor."

"I know," I murmured. "How are you doing?"

"Fine." She looked down at her lap. "Is it wrong to say that I'm relieved? Even if she were here, she wouldn't be *here*, she'd be out getting trashed, or whatever. I always had to clean her up when she came home."

"Nothing you feel is wrong," I assured her, closing my eyes. "How's the book?"

200

"Almost done, actually," she said, and I perked up.

"Really?!" I asked, pulling away to grin down at her. "That's awesome!"

"Yeah, it's almost fifty thousand words." She bit down on her lower lip. "It's so weird... I've never written anything this long before."

"I can't wait to read it." I touched our noses together. "You've kept me waiting long enough."

"I dedicated it to Taylor," Clara said. "Do you think she'll be mad that I added her in?"

"Nah," I said, planting a kiss on her cheek. "What'd you write about her?"

"Some of the stuff before the '*incident*'. She was already using then, but I wrote that she stopped afterwards."

"Did she really?" I asked, cocking my head at her. "At all?"

"Some." Clara shrugged. "She always used to eat popcorn when she was high, and I used to wake up in the middle of the night to the crackling of the microwave from downstairs. After the '*incident*', though, she felt so bad that she hadn't been there with me when it happened that she quit cold-turkey. I'd walk in on her wiping the sweat from her brow, or devouring entire bags of chips, but she always played it off and told me not to worry. A few weeks later, I heard the popping again."

My heart was in my throat. "You have such a way with words."

"I ought to, it's the only thing I'm good at," she laughed.

"That's not true." I pulled her onto my lap, my gaze running over the little freckles dotted across her cheeks and nose.

"Taylor felt bad about not being there for me, and I know she'll feel bad forever," Clara went on, resting her forehead against mine. "But it doesn't matter. I have you. You're there for me, and I love you."

I never told her about the phone call in January, but I had a feeling she knew, anyway.

"I'll be here forever, Clara," I said truthfully, and we kissed.

finale

In a world of color, we sometimes find ourselves overlooking things.

We met in an ice cream shop.

"Two small vanillas, please," said the girl in front of her, knocking once on the counter. My eyes flickered briefly to the brown-haired girl's face, but she was hidden in the shadow of her sister, overlooked by everyone, even myself.

As I talked and laughed and fell in love with the wrong person, Clara drifted over to a table in the corner, hiding behind her hair as she pretended to like vanilla ice cream, pretended to like being there, being civil with the person that had caused her so much pain and hardship, the person that stole so many gazes and tossed them away as if they meant nothing.

I watched them as they finished their ice cream, watched them as they left the store, watched them as they got in their white truck and drove away. That day, my life changed forever, but not because of the girl with the purple hair and the loud, bold laugh.

It was in that ice cream shop that I met the love of my life.

I just didn't see her right away.

the end

acknowledgements

Writing a book is a very personal process. It's easy for me to get sucked into the idea that I did this all by myself, motivated solely by my own interests, and that everyone around me only served as obstacles on the path to completion. I took some time to reflect on the months I spent writing *See Her* a few years ago, and found that the self-absorbed notion of independence couldn't be farther from the truth.

Firstly, my parents were crucial in the development and deliverance of *See Her*. They provided me with my tools, supported me, and put up with my endless demands and compulsive perfectionism. Thank you for being so patient.

As ridiculous as it sounds (even to my own ears) I do have to thank Sebastian Stan for acting as the primary motivation for the majority of this book. Sebastian is a celebrity that has appeared in many films and, of course, has no idea that I exist. A few months before I began See Her, I learned I was going to get the opportunity to meet him in person, and I wanted to try something different than what I'd seen other fans do for him. Writing is what I do, so I set out to create this book for Sebastian, and managed to complete it just days before I presented it to him at the convention. He still continues to inspire me in many ways, and without his presence in my life, *See Her* would not have been completed as quickly; perhaps it would not have been completed at all.

Writing *See Her* for Sebastian set me on a pattern to create novels dedicated to all my favorite celebrities, which soon became a core characteristic for my brand as an author. I'm grateful that I got to meet him.

See Her has accumulated hundreds of thousands of views on my online Wattpad profile, and I'm overwhelmingly thankful for my fans and supporters for giving me the confidence I needed to publish this book. Without them, I would be a vastly different person than I am today, and I thank them a thousand times over for shaping me into a better person and author. I hope I make you proud.

Finally, I'd like to give a nod to everyone who contributed to the late-stage edits of *See Her*, including, but not limited to: my editor(s), for helping me produce the best version possible—Isabel Burke, for designing the cover—and my tech support, who allowed me to design *See Her* to my own specifications and likeness.

When I was in the second grade, I remember creating an "Acknowledgements" chapter for my first (ten-chapter) "novel", *A Friendship Adventure*. I've come a long way from thanking my Polly Pockets and stuffed teddy bear, and would like to finish by reminding anyone reading this to never give up. I've seen far too many careers cut short because people don't get the immediate results they desire. Trust the process. Be kind to yourself and your mistakes.

Thank you.

Jane Cooper (pen name Jane Conquest) is a seventeen-year-old Austin-based writer, illustrator, photographer and more. She is best known for her popular Wattpad profile, JaneConquest-Backup.

Jane is a four-time novelist and aspiring YouTube personality. She plans to pursue writing as a career, and hopes to go to college after high school.

www.janeconquest.com

50847656R00117

Made in the USA
Columbia, SC
11 February 2019